T0274595

Finding Grace

Finding Grace

by

Mary-Lynn Murphy

ScrivenerPress

Library and Archives Canada Cataloguing in Publication

Murphy, Mary-Lynn, 1957-
    Finding Grace / Mary-Lynn Murphy.

ISBN 978-1-896350-52-3

    I. Title.

PS8626.U7579F55 2013   C813'.6   C2013-901763-1

Book design: Laurence Steven
Cover design: Chris Evans
Cover photo: Terry Manzo
Author photo: Jennifer Inglis

Published by Scrivener Press
465 Loach's Road,
Sudbury, Ontario, Canada, P3E 2R2
info@yourscrivenerpress.com
www.scrivenerpress.com

We acknowledge the financial support of the Canada Council for the Arts and the Ontario Arts Council for our publishing activities.

For Ken

ACKNOWLEDGEMENTS

First, I would like to thank Ken Baldwin, for everything.

Thanks also to Laurence Steven at Scrivener Press for his vision and commitment. To Mimi Marrocco for guidance and encouragement. And to the following people for their important contributions to this process: Fran Aspinall, Laura Atkinson, Judy Baldwin, Joan Baril, Karen Barsanti, Barbara Bennett, Earl Blaney, Linda Cheley, Crystal Currie, Mark Dunn, Ted Fryia, Jeff Hinich, Jenn Inglis, Peggy Lauzon, Terry Manzo, Angela Marrocco, Mark McElrea, Simon Melbourne, Mary-Lou Morassut, Michaela Murphy, Rick Sowerby, Joe Sufady, Liza Suhanic, Paul Thompson, Jo Tickle, Gerry Wilson, and Michael Young.

A special thank-you to my mother, Dorothy Murphy. And to my late father, Terry Murphy, who taught me that language matters.

I gratefully acknowledge the assistance of the Ontario Arts Council.

Iris

SOME LIVES CAN'T BE LIVED IN FIRST PERSON. It's too risky. An "I" has to think and act, speak aloud. Better to shrink so far into yourself that you disappear.

Above all, relinquish memory. The dead baby in the toilet, my mother's granite face when I told her. The damp newspaper bundle stuffed into brown paper bags and then into the garbage, her only words to me forged of iron: "You didn't see anything. You will never tell that lie again."

Memory is lava: unpredictable, dangerous. My sister would have done better to forget. Instead she chose the razor edge of memory, the razor's thin white heat against her wrist. Her blood hotter than lava, faster. Stains our mother could not wash out, our father could not deny.

My mother on her knees in the bathroom, pink rag smearing red spatters on the tub, the walls. A moth in my chest, battering its wings against my ribs as I stand in the doorway. "What are you—"

"Your sister did something stupid."

The moth larger, frantic now. "Is she—is she—"

"She's at the hospital. Now go and peel the potatoes for supper."

On the winter ground outside, red stains like small poppies in white snow.

Grace

THE SKY IS HEAVY AND LOW, A GREY WOOL BLANKET with its corners pegged into the ground. Something keeps the rest of the blanket aloft, but just barely. It's the rooftops and the trees holding it up. Even the air smells like wet wool.

Grace is sitting on the front step, examining her wrists and the backs of her hands, which are furred by the fine mist in the air: tiny individual droplets have settled on the hairs on her skin, and she's amused that the overall effect is a pale fur.

She imagines having a luxurious pelt, like a bear or a wolverine or a lynx. How her skin would feel beneath it when she walked in the bush and brushed against tree branches. The velvety protection it would provide, everything sensed through that buffer. How it would feel to curl up in sleep, the softness and warmth of her own hide, like having a built-in comforter. She likes the idea. Even just sitting as she is now, she'd have a thick felt to cushion her butt on the damp concrete. It would be like living inside a marshmallow.

Well, not really; that's taking it a bit far. She shakes the marshmallow analogy, the sticky fake puffiness of it, and snuggles back into the real, 100% animal fur she's just grown, sitting there on her front step, the fog a world in which anything is possible.

Imagining the fur makes her think about how far we've come. Only slightly furred now, walking on two legs, though once we swam in a primordial sea—before we traded gills for lungs. She knows it didn't happen all at once like that, as if fish suddenly morphed into humans. But it's the long-term developments of life on earth that are most enthralling. If only she could have been there to see it all! To watch everything that happened after earth's matter coalesced around an axis and started to spin, held in the magnetic embrace of a powerful star. She'd like to show up sometime in the Precambrian Era to see the earth spit fire and gas from cracks in its crust. And then have a time-lapse experience, to watch lava bubble up and form volcanic cones. And to witness land masses drift apart and re-form into the continents we're familiar with today. Imagine watching the earth's crust wrinkle and fold up into mountains as India crashed into Asia: the birth of the Himalayas. The noise of that! Audible on the next planet! All that massive shifting and drifting, and the chaos of currents in the oceans as huge landmasses set sail for other hemispheres.

What really gets her is the first of everything. The first bit of life in the ocean: a little algae materializing—out of what? The first plant material to colonize a dusty crevice in bare, black rock. Where did it come from? She wants to be the first seed to parachute in on a bit of fluff over that landscape: what would she see? What would that first seed think—if a seed could think, of course—what would it think about its prospects, the earth still burping steam, still cooling down after the trauma of its birth.

That seed would probably wonder what it was doing there on earth. And how it was ever going to get along, fulfill its purpose. Root itself, unfurl stem and leaf, and bloom.

The marine creatures coming ashore is the best part. Whatever possessed them to leave their watery worlds and flop onto lichen-rough rock? It's her time-lapse brain at work again; she knows it didn't happen just like that. But here she goes. She's drifting around at the edge of an ocean, and a wave pushes her up on shore. She gasps, then the ocean reclaims her with another wave. This happens so many times that eventually cells and tissues inside her change so that one time when she's tossed ashore and gasps, oxygen finds its way into her bloodstream. Wow! It's not so bad up here after all, she'd say. Maybe I'll have a little look around. But fins, she'd discover, are not so great for maneuvering in this realm, so her cells and tissues would spend a few more millennia mulling over the problem and eventually solve it by transforming fins into legs.

Think about the story of Noah and the ark. All the creatures rescued from the flood waters. It must be a very old, old story—almost as ancient as the earth. Maybe it's really a story about how we came ashore.

It's those major transformations that are most interesting—the adaptations required for creatures to move from one element into another. That's why amphibians are so fascinating. They embody that transition from something aquatic to something terrestrial. They seem to hover on the verge, members of two realms simultaneously. Imagine being able to breathe through skin, like a frog. Inhaling through all that surface area: the oxygen rush you'd get! She sits very still, closes her eyes, and inhales slowly, her entire body a lung, her skin sieving damp air in through every pore.

Iris

THEY ARRIVED AT DAWN. IT WAS ELEANOR'S IDEA, the day before, to be first on the ice, just the two of them. The sun a red ball rising through the bare arms of the maples. Smoke from the chimneys of nearby houses streamed straight up into the pale sky. The only sound their skate blades scrafing the ice.

Eleanor was about twelve, three years older than Iris. She was quiet that morning, skating round and round the outer edge of the rink as if the younger sister wasn't there. Iris couldn't keep up with her, so she asked Eleanor to help her practise figure eights. Eleanor kept skating. "You look like Barbara Ann Scott," Iris called out, trying to break the spell her sister was under. She grabbed the back of Eleanor's sweater and held on, saying she was a caboose. Wanting to lure Eleanor out of her silence, make her smile. Finally, after purposely stumbling and falling while attempting crossovers, she got Eleanor to snap out of it a bit and coach her. The air held onto Eleanor's words, white vapour, for seconds only.

They had a small back yard, a mostly bald patch of hard-packed earth where even the weeds struggled to survive. A dilapidated wooden fence separated the yard from the train track that ran behind it. In the corner at the end of the driveway was a derelict garage that functioned as a shed. Their father had reinforced the sagging roof with a post erected beneath the ridgepole in the centre of the building. He had also rigged up a kind of refrigerator in there that he built from a small hot water tank he brought home from the dump. After removing a vertical section of the tank's exterior, he installed shelves inside it. He dug a hole in the shed's dirt floor deep enough to sink the tank into, then rigged up a pulley system for lifting it out to get the root vegetables or butter stored inside it. The shed also housed old tools— shovels, a cross-cut saw, a couple of axes. Coils of wire hung on nails. A heavy, rough-hewn workbench ran along the back wall; below it were scattered several battered metal pails and odds and ends of rough lumber. In the corner next to the workbench was an old rattan chair, and along the side wall stood a long, low wooden bench covered with a strip of worn carpet, almost wide enough for a person to sleep on. A small, filmy window above the workbench admitted light, as did the double wooden doors that swung outward and the narrow gaps in the walls where sheathing boards didn't quite meet. In the winter, snow filtered in through the gaps and formed small, arrowed drifts on the benches and shelves and on the floor.

One afternoon Iris wandered into the cool twilight of the shed and found Eleanor hunched in the chair, apparently staring at nothing. Slivers of light slanted in between the sheathing boards, fracturing her face.

"Hey, you look like a zebra," Iris giggled.

Eleanor didn't move. Not an eyelash. Iris noticed a dusty cobweb wavering in the air in front of her sister—the thing that seemed to have her mesmerized.

"Eleanor…" Still no answer. "You're not invisible, you know; I can see you. Stop pretending." Iris was spooked. She wanted to shake her sister. Instead, she took the battered stump of a broom from the corner and brushed the cobweb away. Eleanor's eyes moved; she looked at Iris. Or through her.

"Come on, Eleanor. What are you doing?" Iris used the broom to brush at Eleanor's feet. "Here, I'll clean your shoes." Willing her to smile, speak, return to her body. More and more often Iris was finding her in this state: here in the shed, and in their bedroom, where Eleanor would lie beneath the covers, curled in a tight ball like the shells Iris would find on the beach, brittle and empty. Iris couldn't budge her, couldn't make Eleanor unwind her tightly coiled body.

Who could she tell? Not her parents—her mostly absent father and her mother, the perpetual-motion machine stuck on one setting: brusque. "You don't have to tell me about it," she said the one time Iris brought it up. "I've had enough of her moping around, looking for attention. Just ignore her."

≈

After the first time, when she got home from the hospital, Eleanor stayed in bed, not talking to anybody. Their mother told Iris to leave her alone. For two days she did. She'd creep out of their room in the morning and creep back into it at bedtime. She was worried about saying or doing the wrong thing, not knowing what made Eleanor take a razor to her wrists in the first place.

But the third day, Iris peeked into the dim room after school. Eleanor was lying in bed with her face to the wall. Iris couldn't tell if she was awake or asleep. It didn't matter. She walked quietly into the room, closing the door behind her. She hesitated beside the bed, listened for the sound of Eleanor's breathing. The white chenille bedspread that covered her body rose and fell ever so slightly. Iris whispered, "Hi Eleanor, it's me." Then she climbed onto the bed and lay down beside her, on top of the blankets. Eleanor was lying on her side and so did Iris, facing her sister's back, trying not to disturb her. But close enough that she'd feel Iris was there. Iris's breathing fell in with Eleanor's. After a while, Iris inched over so she was almost touching Eleanor, who shifted slightly then, as if she was just letting her body relax. Just enough that her back settled in against Iris, nestling into the curve of her body. They lay like that a long while.

At mealtimes Iris would bring two plates into the bedroom. After a few days, she got Eleanor to sit up and eat with her. And gradually Iris started to beat back the silence with stories from school and the neighbourhood. Old Mrs. Harris chasing the Kelly boys out of her yard with a shotgun after they'd been throwing snowballs at her windows. "Do you think it was loaded?" Iris asked, using questions to lure Eleanor into conversation. Iris talked about Walter Davies going off to fight in Korea. "Where *is* Korea, anyway?" Eventually Eleanor agreed to go outside and push Iris on the old swing that hung from the maple tree. The snow was gone by then but the leaves weren't out yet, so sunlight glared off everything—the fence, the smooth grey branches of the tree, the old shed with its peeling white paint. While they were out there, their father emerged from the shed, stood with a hand shading his eyes and looked their way. "You girls having fun?"

"Yeah—except Eleanor stopped pushing," Iris said, craning her neck around to see what Eleanor was doing. She was just standing there like she was frozen, staring at the ground. "Come on, El," Iris called out, "I'm slowing down!" Their father wandered back into the shed. "It's better when you keep pushing, come on," Iris called behind her.

Eleanor still wasn't moving.

"Do you want a turn now?" Iris asked.

She just stared at the shed, shaking her head no.

$\approx$

It was the autumn Iris had started high school. When she got home one afternoon, her mother was muttering about how Eleanor was not around to help with supper and was likely lolling about somewhere. She sent Iris to the shed to get carrots and turnips from the refrigerator.

The late October wind strummed the bare branches of the maples—a faraway sound, like ghosts moaning about the cold. Spent leaves whirled up toward the sky, as if to find the branches from which they'd fallen. Both of the wide garage doors were closed, which was odd; usually one of them was left ajar until the snow came, after which the family used the man-door at the side of the shed. Iris decided to pull open one of the big doors to let in more light. It lurched as the bottom of it caught on the ground, dragging bits of dirt and leaves with it. She stepped inside, smelling the familiar earthy must of the place. The pallid light that washed in through the entranceway caught something near the low bench along the side wall. A slump of rags, a doll? Larger. An arm stretched out to one side, resting on the floor. The dirt floor, dark with tar, paint, something spilled. Thunder somewhere, everywhere, pushing against her chest, pounding the interior walls of the shed. Shadows and grey light: a black-and-white film, even the blood that had leaked from Eleanor's wrists looked black, the blood on Iris's hands, her open mouth a dark oval emptying the word *No* into the jabbering air.

≈

How absence can consume so much space in a person. I felt hollowed out, cored. Into the hole at the centre of me went everything: words especially. Nothing warranted the immense effort required to press tongue against teeth or palate and give them breath. It was something my mother couldn't force me to do. She couldn't slap words out of me, or badger them out or auger them out with her glare. Speaking was unnecessary. Writing was sufficient to complete my schoolwork; the teacher had no more power over my voice than my mother.

My silence was a comforting embrace, wrapping its arms around that space Eleanor had disappeared into, holding her in, preventing her from evaporating.

The last word I spoke for five years was *No*. A word whose shape is a hole, a word that can swallow you. A pebble tossed into a canyon.

I woke in the night and saw the shape of a body in Eleanor's bed. *She's back!* I stepped across the floor, one arm extended. Just as my hand reached the blanket, Mother startled awake with a grunt and sat up. Eleanor's name was caught in my throat, snagged there, a knot of brambles. My mother was cross. "Go back to sleep." I stood beside the bed, whimpering, kneading the blankets, shivering as if winter had inhabited me. She tugged the bedding out of my hands. "Stop your snivelling and go back to sleep—now."

Eleanor and I had been like two sailors trapped on a ghost-ship drifting through fog. We'd kept each other company since our parents could not—were not equipped for the emotional voyage of parenting.

And I ended up just like them.

Religion wasn't a big deal in our household when I was growing up. We went to an Anglican church now and then: Christmas, Easter. No funeral for my sister. No wake, no church service, no casket or body. No evidence of failure or shame. From the shed to the morgue. From there to a hole in the ground.

Gone.

I was bleeding words in my dreams. As I spoke, words the colour of blood hung in the air an instant before dissolving into drops that spilled down my blouse, dripped onto the floor. But I couldn't stop speaking; the words pulsed out as if I'd severed an artery in my mouth. Each utterance a red bloom suspended in the air before it melted and fell, staining my clothes, the floor, my shoes. Suddenly it wasn't me, it was Eleanor trying to speak with a mouth full of blood and a look of shock on her face, her two cupped hands coming up to her lips, blood streaming through her fingers. Then I was awake, my heart thundering in my chest and that pebble, *No*, caught in my throat.

Grace

GRACE IS OUTSIDE LISTENING TO THAT HIGH TINKLING sound of earth sipping snow-melt. She grins, imagining the ground beneath her feet suddenly rippling with the movement of a million small mouths sipping and slurping, a barely audible sigh of satisfaction as the earth's thirst is quenched. After a few minutes, she lifts her head, listens to the wind. Smaller branches crackle and creak, working the winter out of their joints. Seasonal yoga; salutation to the spring, not just the dawn. Kaia has tried to teach her some yoga moves, but Grace just can't be serious about it all, especially because of the names. When she hears "downward-facing dog," she pictures a basset hound on a yoga mat, trying to get its rear end up into the air, elegantly. She sees his blood-shot eyes, a hound dog with a hangover trying to be all earnest about his yoga practice.

Grace shakes her head, snickering. She spies a jack pine cone on the grass and picks it up. It looks like a Shriner's slipper with its pointy turned-up tip. She runs her finger along the bumpy surface of the cone. It's glued shut with a kind of resin that melts when it gets hot enough, like in a forest fire. Then the bracts can open and release the seeds.

But the real magic starts with germination. She's a seed in the dark soil, noticing something seeping down into the dirt. Hmmm, it's getting a bit damp here, I wonder… PING! Out pops a little root. Oh my, that's interesting; it's like a straw for sipping good stuff out of the soil. Ooh, another strange sensation—like I think I might sneeze—ah!

Something else popped out and it's wanting to unfurl, there it goes up through the dirt, and oh! I think it's broken through the surface!

That's the best part, when it breaks through the soil. It's always amazing to see a tender green shoot that has speared through an old dead leaf on the ground, so intent is it on making its way to the light.

She wanders over to the edge of the bush. Hears the high two-note spring song of the chickadees, staking out their territory. Mr. and Mrs. Humphries taught her that birds have all kinds of vocalizations that mean different things: territorial songs; warning calls; other calls to let the members of their flock know where they are—like saying *I'm over here! Yoo-hoo, now I'm in this other tree! Now I'm in the next tree over!* Imagine if people did that; we'd drive each other crazy.

Some people *are* like that, though. Like Shelley Edwards who comes into the library just to talk, it seems. She's like the red-eyed vireo that never shuts up, going on and on about what her sister thinks about the colour of the door on her neighbour's house, and what her daughter's up to these days down in Mississauga where they have a nice new shopping mall. Then there are the people who are completely the opposite, who look like they will kill you if you say one word to them. Either that or they will run away and throw themselves into the river, as if the sound of a human voice is more than they can bear. There's one guy in town who has that look about him. Wild-animal timid. She doesn't know if he can talk, wonders if he'd run from the sound of his own voice.

Imagine being spooked by that, the sound of your own voice.

She's over at the garden now, admiring the crocuses newly emerged from beneath the snow. They're not sure, either, about their own voices at first. They kind of stammer a bit till the sun finds them. Then they open their throats wide and let the light pour out.

Iris

SHE BEGAN TO INCH HER WAY BACK INTO THE WORLD. Through fog, through cotton batting. At school, her wooden desk with its round hole in the upper right-hand corner, for the inkwell. But it was math class and she was gripping a pencil. A blank page in front of her. She moved the pencil, made a short vertical line. The number 1, or a small letter l, or a capital I, it could have been any of those, or the beginning of something. The first stroke in a capital E. The name Eleanor: she made it appear on the page. Then she turned the pencil over, used the pink rubber end of it to make the word disappear. In its place, pink eraser crumbs; somehow that scatter of crumbs held the puzzle of her sister's name. She started again with the single vertical pencil stroke, built from it the word Iris, then transformed it into pink crumbs too. She peered at the eraser end of the pencil. Part of it had also disappeared. She rubbed the eraser across the blank page until there was nothing left of the pink nub, until the metal cylinder holding it tore through the paper.

At first she couldn't make eye contact with anyone at school. Nobody knew what to do or say, not even her good friends. Except for Dorothy Sanders, who was brave enough to write Iris a note.

> *I'm sorry about your sister. I know you don't like talking now, but I like writing and receiving notes, so we could "talk" on paper if you like.*
>
> Your friend,
> Dorothy Sanders

It meant she wouldn't drown.

Dorothy even managed to get Iris to come over to her house sometimes after school, and often on Saturdays they'd walk downtown. She became good at using yes/no questions to shape a conversation, and over time the two of them developed a kind of sign language. But Iris wasn't very good company, and after about a year, Dorothy started hanging around with a larger group of girls and guys. At first she'd invite Iris to come along, but Iris never did, and the invitations ceased. When she was almost sixteen, Iris and her parents moved to the other side of town to a bigger house so they could take in boarders. Her mother needed her help more regularly, and this ended Iris's relationship with Dorothy.

Within a year of their starting the boarding house, a young fellow named Hal moved in. Not too much older than Iris. Movie-star handsome, with dark hair, soft brown eyes and thick eyelashes. She was drawn not just to his beauty but to the sadness in his eyes, and to his silence: at the breakfast and dinner table, he was almost as mute as she was.

On one of his days off, Hal returned to the boarding house in the late afternoon, after a couple of hours at the Milltown Tavern. Iris was cleaning the front hall, dusting the banister and balusters on the staircase leading to the second floor. The hall was separated from the living room and the rest of the main floor by a pair of French doors that were ajar. When Hal came in through the front door, Iris was at the base of the stairs. The two of them paused for a moment and looked at each other, then away. Hal glanced toward the living room, listened. Then their eyes met again, and he said, "Always working." Iris smiled shyly, shrugged.

"Your parents home?"

She shook her head no, motioned with her arm that they were out.

"Home all alone."

She nodded, playing with the dust rag in her hands, twisting and untwisting it. That sensation in her thighs, something between an ache and a tremor, as if her legs were about to give way.

"How old are you?"

She smiled, looked at her shoes.

"Old enough for a boyfriend?" He walked to where she stood at the bottom of the stairs. A delicious tension in the air, their eyes holding and then releasing. He pushed a hand through his hair, scanned the living room and hallway. Then he ran his palm down her forearm until her hand rested in his. He squeezed it lightly. "Old enough to kiss a boy?" Aiming to sound mischievous, confident, but his voice was too soft for that, his eyes serious above the crooked line of his lips. Even alcohol could not lighten him.

Then they were kissing, uncertain at first, until they responded to their bodies' teaching and let their mouths soften, their tongues and hands explore. They were learning fast, in the front hall of the house presided over by Iris's stern mother, who entered the back door into the kitchen noisily enough to be heard by Hal and Iris. They pulled apart as Mrs. Mitchell called Iris's name a second time. Hal disappeared up the stairs as Iris recovered her dusting cloth and coughed.

Silence from the kitchen, followed by Mrs. Mitchell's heavy tread across the living room floor, her appearance in the doorway to the hall. She looked at Iris, up the stairs, and back at her daughter. Iris lamely moved the rag along the banister, then looked ever so casually at her mother.

During the evening meal, Mrs. Mitchell's purposeful eyes shifted around the table until she had all the evidence she needed. Iris dropped cutlery twice, and when she placed a serving dish on the table near Hal, she almost flinched as if she'd been burned. Hal, who was normally quiet at the table anyway, kept his eyes glued to his plate as if it was the only thing keeping him from spinning into outer space.

"Hal, another helping of potatoes?" Mrs. Mitchell asked, resting her eyes on him. He met her gaze briefly and accepted the offer of extra food, the first time he'd ever heard her invite her boarders to eat more.

Iris thought her mother would never leave her alone in the house again on Hal's day off, but she was wrong. At breakfast the next week, Mrs. Mitchell made a point of saying that she was going out for a few hours, and asked Iris to clean the upstairs bedrooms and bathroom. She indicated to the boarders that they should vacate the house while Iris did her chores.

This scenario repeated itself for a couple of weeks, and each time, Mrs. Mitchell returned at the designated hour. But the third week, she came home early enough to find Iris and Hal in the middle of what Mrs. Mitchell called dishonourable conduct, after which she suggested that Hal could redeem her daughter's honour by marrying her. Iris was seventeen.

≈

I was hungry in a house of scarcity. Hal's eyes on me, and then his mouth, his hands—for the first time I knew what feasting was. I was gluttonous. All I wanted was that physicality, our bodies bound together in a kind of joint agony. And then losing myself in those waves that rolled through me. It wasn't chemistry, which implies a reaction between two people—something shared. It was physics: moving body parts in such a way as to achieve the desired result: temporary, blissful amnesia.

≈

Was she in love with him? She won't say. But look at her there, her legs wrapped tightly around him. He's what's anchoring her to the earth. Shaping her, giving shape to her days.

Isn't that the same as love?

If he'd been a different sort of man, he could have drawn words out of her. If he'd been less encumbered by his own demons. If he'd been as able to be kind as Dorothy Sanders.

If.

He wasn't unkind. He just wasn't present. Even after lovemaking: Iris tried to curl into the crook of his arm, lay her head on his chest. Listen to his heart, an animal galloping away. Or if she was on top of him, she'd peer into his face. What was she searching for? Something in his eyes that would reflect her back, delineate her.

But he wouldn't maintain eye contact. He'd clear his throat, shift the weight of her off him, and get out of bed. Pull on his pants and leave the bedroom.

One of the first times he did this, she followed him to the kitchen. He was sitting in a chair, faintly illuminated by light from the bathroom. His hand rested on the table, around a bottle of beer. She stood in the doorway in her robe, her cocked head posing a question.

He glanced up at her and then away. His voice was gentle enough. "You should go back to bed."

More and more often, even when he was working day shift, he didn't come home for supper. Most evenings seemed to unfold in the same way. She had the table set: two placemats, two plates, the cutlery arranged the way her mother had taught her, two glasses. On top of the stove, a casserole getting cold. She sat at the table and watched daylight falter. Turned on the overhead light, scooped a spoonful of food onto her plate. Chewed and swallowed, noticing how the flowers didn't match up at the wallpaper seams.

When he came home a couple hours later, he wasn't drunk enough to miss the puffy redness around her eyes. He muttered an apology, told her he met some of the boys at the Legion after work.

"Don't wait for me at supper, if I'm not home. Just go ahead and eat."
He turned on the radio to diminish the silence.

She went into the bedroom, lay on the bed and stared at the ceiling, at the fine web of cracks in the plaster.

It was better when he worked evening shifts; then she set just one place at the table, and his absence didn't feel like a slap. She was in bed when he got home, whether it was immediately after his shift or hours later. He could crawl into bed in the dark, without disturbing her. Or he could start at her ankles and work his way up, waking her with his touch or his tongue. It was always better this way.

But one night, when Hal arrived late after a day shift, something new entered their life together. She opened and slammed every cupboard door in the kitchen, then whirled around, lifted an empty glass from the table, and hurled it at the wall just beside his head. He flinched, yelled *What the fuck—?* as she stormed into the bedroom and slammed the door behind her.

It was like a feast, this rage. It filled her to the brim with something she hadn't tasted before.

Mrs. Baxter

I DIDN'T KNOW WHAT TO THINK THAT FIRST TIME I MET THEM. Not one peep out of her, and he didn't say more'n a few words. They were new in town, looking at the apartment we had for rent upstairs. I told them about it being furnished and all, found myself chattering away to try to get them to soften up, say a word or two. They barely looked at me. He kept his eyes moving around the place as if he was trying to sniff out a ghost. She watched him, and now and then she'd reach out her hand to touch the table, a chair, the counter. She opened a couple of kitchen cupboards, and when I caught her eye, tried to smile. A pitiful sight, really. Hal asked me again about the price; after I told him, he glanced at her and she shrugged. So he said, "We'll take it." I never heard one word from her the whole time, and told my husband afterwards that I didn't know if she was shy or just plain rude.

Turns out, as I learned after they moved in, she didn't speak, ever. Dumb but not deaf; I don't know how that works. She just looked out of those blue eyes at you, as if she was down at the bottom of a lake, staring up through water.

I worried about the young bride, all alone in her life, it seemed, except for that glum husband of hers. I started dropping in on her, making excuses, saying could I borrow an egg when I had half a dozen in the fridge downstairs. It's hard to make conversation with some- body who don't say a word, but we managed with my bits of prattle and her nodding, even sometimes almost smiling.

She was getting a bit round in the belly, it seemed to me, and bigger in the chest, but she wasn't giving me any sign language about a baby. After she was getting more comfortable with me, I took the plunge one day. I nodded toward her expanding belly, smiled and said, "So have we got a wee one on the way, then?" I thought my eyes was sparkly enough—a happy expression, so as not to frighten her. But the look of startlement that came over her face.

"Now, now," I said to her. "It's all right. It's just the normal course of things, to have a baby come along after you're married." But her eyes wouldn't settle down. She shook her head ever so slightly, raised her shoulders as if to say, "I'm not sure."

It was clear this girl didn't know anything.

I reached across and patted her knee. "How long—how many months since your last monthly?" She glanced off to the side, thinking. Then held up four fingers. "That means you're four months pregnant." I was trying to keep my voice calm, not show the shock of it, this girl out in the world with no idea. "You'll be having a baby in another five months," I smiled. "Isn't that wonderful!" She just sat there staring at me. Then she looked down, lifted her hand up from her lap, and rested her palm on her belly, circling it lightly. I was waiting for a smile. But she just looked at me again.

"Don't you worry," I told her. "I had two babies of my own. I'll be here to help you along." She was younger than my own two sons. Well Lord, I thought, I guess you've sent me that daughter I wanted.

I'd been telling her about my church for awhile, inviting her to come with me on Sundays. Now I became a bit more insistent. "There's a visiting minister coming this Sunday. He's got the gift of healing, I've seen it. He can help you," I said, touching my throat. "Lord knows you're going to need a voice with a young one around. Come with me on Sunday while that minister is here." She seemed less set against it than all the other times I'd invited her, so I took that as a sign. "I'll come up to get you at 10:30 on Sunday morning." She nodded ever so slightly.

Iris

Mrs. Baxter's church wasn't at all like the Anglican church
Iris's parents took her to now and then when she was a girl. Just a plain
room with chairs set up on either side of a central aisle, facing a lectern. No altar, no kneeling benches. In the front right corner, though,
was a deep, square tank with steps leading to the top of it. Iris learned
later that this was for baptisms.

It was a small congregation, only about thirty people there, but
once the service got going, there was so much energy in the church it
seemed like the room was packed full. There was no choir or organ,
but one fellow led the singing and everyone joined in with gusto, not
just politely murmuring the lyrics, but opening their mouths wide and
pouring out the hymns. "What a Friend We Have in Jesus." "I'll Fly
Away By and By." "There is Power in the Blood." Neither of the minis-
ters wore robes. The regular pastor introduced the visiting evangelist,
a short, fair-haired man who began quietly enough, talking about his
childhood in Ohio and several dissolute years of early adulthood. "In
Jeremiah Chapter 13, the Lord speaks of the people who found grace
in the wilderness, and that was me," he chuckled. "I wandered in the
wilderness for a time before I finally heeded the call of the Lord."

He talked on, quoting from Jeremiah. "Behold I will bring them
from the north country, and gather them from the coasts of the earth,
and with them the blind and the lame, the woman with child and her
that travaileth with child together." Then he veered off into interpreta-
tion, becoming more animated as he continued, his voice rising, then

dropping into stillness, then climbing again, like a kite that sails and then suddenly dips and plummets until it catches another updraft. He'd left his notes and the lectern by now and was pacing back and forth in front of the chairs, his voice rising in a crescendo. "The Lord said, They shall COME with WEEPING, and I WILL LEAD them. I will TURN THEIR MOURNING INTO JOY!"

Abruptly he stopped and smiled, the spell broken. He calmly said, "Halleluiah," and the congregants called out Amen, and Halleluiah, and Thank you Jesus. Back at the lectern again, the minister stood a moment grinning at the people sitting before him, some with arms raised toward the ceiling. "Praise God," he said, and started again in his calm voice talking about some people not wanting to hear the call, some taking longer to hear it. Like family members. "The Lord heard the lamentation of Rahel because her children refused to be comforted, they refused to come into the fold. But God told Rahel, Refrain thy voice from weeping, and thine eyes from tears: for THY WORK SHALL BE RE-WARDED and they shall COME AGAIN from the LAND OF THE ENEMY." He dwelled awhile on the reference to Rahel's work. "It's part of your ministry, to help them awaken to the voice of God—all people, but especially your families, your loved ones." His voice was increasing in intensity again, his index finger jabbing the air. "Because EVERYONE who IS NOT SAVED shall DIE for his OWN INIQUITY! BEHOLD, the WHIRL-WIND OF THE LORD goeth FORTH with a FURY!" He was stalking across the front of the room again, then turned with his Bible raised in both hands and shouted, "IT SHALL FALL WITH PAIN UPON THE HEAD OF THE WICKED!" as he slammed the Bible down on an imaginary head.

This time there was no break in the intensity with which he spoke. Words poured out of him, the word of God mixed in with his own, his whole body engaged in the delivery of his message. "Turn away from evil, make your ways and doings good. And if you do, he will bless you. God WANTS to bless you. He says I am WITH thee to SAVE thee, I will HEAL thee OF THY WOUNDS." He'd loosened his tie, and his blond hair looked white in contrast to the deep red of his face and neck. The Lamentations, he was saying. "He hath SET me in DARK PLACES, he hath HEDGED me about, that I CANNOT GET OUT: he hath MADE my CHAIN HEAVY. But, the Lord is MERCIFUL to THOSE WHO SEEK him, those who REPENT and FOLLOW his RIGHTEOUS PATH. Jeremiah says Let us SEARCH and TURN AGAIN to the Lord. Let us LIFT UP OUR HEART WITH OUR HANDS UNTO GOD IN THE HEAVENS!"

People were standing now, arms raised skyward, swaying back and forth, some muttering incomprehensibly as the minister continued. "I CALLED UPON THY NAME, oh Lord, out of the LOW DUNGEON. Thou hast HEARD MY VOICE: HIDE NOT THINE EAR FROM MY CRY. God WANTS to MAKE you WHOLE! Jesus is HERE with us today, this MINUTE. He is in this ROOM! The power of the Holy Spirit is STRONG in this room. I feel his POWER moving through me, his HEALING POWER! Come up to the front all those who seek God's healing power; COME UP, COME UP and receive the GIFT OF THE HOLY SPIRIT!"

The man who had been leading the singing started up with "Amazing Grace." Fifteen or twenty people streamed to the front of the church. The minister continued to gather the force of the Holy Spirit inside him, at first striding back and forth shouting as people sang and swayed and spoke in tongues. Then he went up to a small middle-aged woman at the front of the crowd, tears streaming down her face. He held her head between his hands, spoke vehemently into her face, and then stepped back, raised one arm and brought it swiftly down, his palm lightly striking her forehead. She fell back into the arms of someone waiting there to ease her to the floor. The minister made his way through the crowd like this, someone always there to catch the ones crumpling beneath the force of the spirit.

It was general mayhem, the noise of many voices and many languages rising feverishly, some people twitching on the floor and others lying still, eyes closed. Other members of the congregation, the ones still at their seats, prayed aloud, not in unison, not a prayer from a book, but carrying on their own lively conversations with God, their own bellowed or muttered invocations.

Why did I even agree to go to church with Mrs. Baxter? I was looking for something, but I knew it had to be something outside of me: nothing useful could have come from within me. I wasn't planning to go up front, but Mrs. Baxter took my elbow and herded me out into the aisle, alternately shouting Thank you Jesus and urging in a low, insistent voice, "He can help you, he can heal you, open your heart to the Lord." Before I knew it, I was in that swarm at the front of the church. All those voices everywhere, the cries and tears of ecstasy, the impassioned exhortations of the preacher riding the crest of that wave of emotion. As Mrs. Baxter hovered close behind me, the lobster-red preacher approached, and his hand came down on my head.

It seemed to come from within, as if the kernel of darkness there cracked clean open and a river of light poured out of it, carrying me with it. It lifted my feet off the ground and floated me somewhere outside of myself: somewhere safe. And with that flood of light, a warmth surged through me, pushing up through my throat and out my mouth. The sound of my voice/not my voice, an alien sound. My mouth full of words, then emptying and filling again and again. Unrecognizable words. Nobody, including me, could have understood them.

But of course they would be incomprehensible. How could those years of unspoken sadness, anger and emptiness be filtered through as fine a sieve as words?

After the service, Mrs. Baxter oozed congratulations, patting me on the arm and scrutinizing me as if I might grow a third eye any minute. "There now, you're all better. You were talking away in there, just like the apostles after they received the gift of tongues." She searched my face. "How do you feel?"

The trouble with language is not just the uttering of words—the mechanics or physiology of it. It's a problem of content.

Finding Grace

How do you feel? When you've just experienced the spiritual equivalent of multiple orgasms on a church floor, surrounded by a crowd of others in similar rapture. When you'd been living in a black-and-white world, and a technicolour one comes rushing headlong toward you, so that suddenly you're not inhabiting your own life anymore.

But maybe that was the point—that's where the relief came from: the notion that I didn't have to inhabit that life anymore. I could shed it like a skin.

"How do you feel?"

I croaked out *okay*. Meaning: soft and exposed, the way I did after getting such a severe sunburn as a girl that my skin peeled off in puffy, damp strips, exposing a reptilian-looking layer of newborn skin below.

Mrs. Baxter chattered on about how surprised and happy my husband was going to be, to learn that I had been healed, that I'd found my voice. When I got home, Hal was listening to a ball game on the radio. I ventured over to the set and turned it down. He frowned at me, started to get up out of the chair. I held up my hand and said, "Hello, Hal."

He sat back in his chair, appearing, as Mrs. Baxter had predicted, quite surprised. But more alarmed than happy.

He squinted at me.

"I can talk again." Was I hopeful? How did I think he would react, this man who spoke only slightly more than I did? This man I had never had a conversation with, in the two years we'd lived together.

Margaret

A CRASH, GLASS BREAKING. HER HEART A FIST POUNDING against her breastbone. His voice, the slurry rage in it. She can't make out the words. Her mother's voice, small and hard, spitting stones. Margaret does what she always does: drops out of the warm bed, pulling a blanket with her. Knees on the cold floor. She slides under the bed, dragging the blanket in to cover her. With one eye she watches. She can hear her father's heavy unsteady steps in the hall, his hand trying to find the doorknob. A sudden rectangle of light falls across the floor, framing his shadow before he stumbles into the room.

The empty bed, a lump of blankets on top of it, pose a riddle he can't resolve. He doesn't know exactly why he's in this room, or what he wants. He sits on the floor and leans back against the side of the bed, both legs straight out in front of him, socked feet splayed. His incomprehension leaks out in a stream of muttering, nothing she can make sense of. Then he's quiet for a minute before she hears a series of short, sharp exhales. He's crying.

Margaret doesn't make a sound in her secret nest beneath the bed.

Iris

HAL AND I WERE LIKE TWO MARBLES RATTLING AROUND in an empty drawer. Do you hear the sound those marbles make, rolling randomly about as you open the drawer? Hollow.

For two years, we hadn't been required to make small talk. He never had much to say and seemed relieved by my silence. Would it have been any different if one or both of us had been inclined to converse? What would we have said to each other? How do married people manage to fill all that space between them, when there is an expectation that they speak to one another?

"How was your day, dear?"

"It was fine; how was yours?"

"Mine was fine too."

"The traffic light on Water Street wasn't working this morning."

"I bought each of us a new toothbrush today."

I'm sure that's why people have kids: to interrupt conversations, or what passes for conversation. Something to divert attention from the void between two people tied to each other for life, supposedly. Children provide a topic for conversation slightly more interesting than what otherwise occurs. "The baby threw up on my shoulder, all over my clean sweater."

I thought our child might create a bond between Hal and me. A reason. Lots of people think that about babies, think they'll be an Answer instead of just another of life's complications. But our daughter's presence didn't lessen the silence much, except for her own babbling. I wasn't exactly a Chatty Kathy, and Hal continued to be withdrawn.

Now and then, though, I'd catch him watching her with a faint smile on his face, especially when she was playing by herself and chattering away in an incomprehensible language. One time, she picked up her doll and carried it over to him, thrust it into his hands. "Play," she said, before returning to the blocks on the floor. Hal was startled by this. He shifted the doll from one hand to the other, looking around as if to find an escape route. Then he turned the doll to face him, inspected it, straightened out its pink pyjamas. He held it vertically and then tipped it back horizontally, back and forth like that a few times, watching the doll's eyes open and close.

I called her Margaret. Her second name, Eleanor, was like a secret: her silent name, the name I couldn't bear to use every day.

But I was afraid of her. Afraid of what she stirred in me. Something almost physical. Visceral. The word love, like a crocus beneath the snow, something implausible.

I didn't know what to do with it, this budding feeling. So I did my best to bury it, replace it with something less volatile: duty. Feed, clothe, house; instil the fear of the Lord.

Margaret

AT PENTECOST, WHEN MARGARET IS SIX YEARS OLD, she brings home a picture of her family that she drew at Sunday school. On the page are three figures with round heads and rectangular bodies and limbs. Margaret is standing between her parents, an arm stretched out toward each of them. Her mother's head is ablaze—an orange conflagration, the helmet of hair unmelting beneath the flames. Her father's short, dark hair is represented by heavy black spikes protruding from his scalp. He has not been set alight, but in the background, a house is burning, yellow flames shooting out the windows and the chimney.

In the lower corner of the picture is a fire truck arriving on the scene. Maybe her father called the fire department to douse the flames of the Holy Spirit when It blew in.

Hal

HE's LYING ON THE COUCH AFTER COMING OFF NIGHT SHIFT. As he sleeps soundly, Margaret pulls three chairs over and lines them up in front of the couch. She then makes a tent by draping a blanket across him and the backs of the chairs. Beneath the blanket, in the space between the chairs and the couch, she plays with her doll Sara, the stuffed dog named Puppy, and Teddy the bear. Teddy and Puppy are fighting, and Sara is warning them that they'll get thrown off the boat if Noah hears them. In fact, Sara is about to tell on them. She marches up to Noah's shoulder and informs him, in a high, squeaky voice, about the other two fighting.

Hal feels an insistent nudging at his shoulder. He opens his eyes to see the tented blanket to his right, and hears a high voice emanating from beneath it. He lifts the blanket and peers groggily underneath. Margaret stops talking a second and looks at him. Then she thrusts Sara toward his face and squeaks, "Noah's awake!" Sara turns away from Noah and bounces up and down as she continues to harangue Teddy and Puppy. "See?" she squeals. "Now you woke him up and now he's going to toss you into the water."

"What are you doing under there?"

"Playing Noah Zark."

"Oh." A pause. "Who have you got there?"

"Teddy and Puppy. Sara is Mrs. Zark."

She reads the question in his face. "Mrs. Zark. You know, Noah Zark and Mrs. Zark and all the animals he takes on their boat."

"Oh yeah?" He searches for something else to say. "Then what happens?"

"Then it rains and rains, and there's a flood, and then the dove comes back with leaves in its mouth."

"Ah," he says, and they look at each other. He lets the blanket down again and lies there, an unlikely Noah, waiting for the dove.

Iris

EVERYTHING IS CLEARER LOOKING BACK, and from this remove. There are the lives we think we live and then there are our actual lives, which we can never clearly see until it's too late for the truth to mean anything. What's left then is irony.

What was ironic in my life? That in finding my voice again at that church, the truth of my family story was silenced once and for all. When I'd been mute, I hadn't silenced it; I had merely withdrawn from the telling. But in my Pentecostal fervour, I replaced the real story with something more comforting, more acceptable to a general audience or at least the congregation that became my audience, that gathered round me and lifted me up, that said You Belong Here. A congregation of people whose prayer for deliverance was perhaps like mine: deliver me from my past, and from a fruitless present. Deliver me unto oblivion.

So I gave no breath to secrets from the past, to the emptiness of the present. I smothered all that with prayer. Someone else's words, someone else's story. Anyone's but mine.

I was hell-bent on salvation, and in my mind that meant I had to rescue Hal as well, see our little family transformed into something holy. But he was unsalvageable. And our daughter and he became silent allies, both of them set against me, undermining my efforts to save us all. I was a Christian soldier, armed with belief. Or despair. And they refused to march with me.

Margaret

THE PALE HARD LIGHT OF WINTER BRIGHTENS THE KITCHEN.
Margaret's alone at the table eating breakfast, the back of the cereal
box facing her. The only sound in the kitchen is her spoon in the
bowl, scrape scrape. Down the hall, the shuffle of her father's slippers.
Then he appears, wearing blue striped pyjamas, his red eyes squinting
toward the window. Margaret's spoon scrapes the bowl once, twice.
Their eyes meet.

"What are you eating there?"

"Honeycombs."

"Honeycombs." He chuckles, turns his eyes to the window again.
He looks as if he can't make up his mind about something; his body
shifts slightly as if he might turn to leave, but then he says, "You're
eating Honeycombs, are you?"

"Yeah. They're my favourite."

"They're your favourite, are they?" A crooked smile. He shifts
again. The clock ticks. "Well I'll let you eat your Honeycombs then."
He walks back down the hall. Margaret hears the bathroom door
close. The sound of her spoon in the bowl, almost empty now.

Hal

A LETTER ARRIVES FROM HIS BROTHER, TELLING HIM that their father has died.

That's it, then. A chapter closed.

Not really closed.

Like a gate without a latch: why can't he make it close for good?

His murderous silence. It won't do any good now, to talk about it. He has run the film over again in his mind enough times, trying to play it out differently. In each rerun, he tells the truth.

But what is truth?

It's the punch in the gut that folds you in two.

All those years; that man hanging for Hal's sin. To speak now…

To speak: to open. Mouth, arms, heart. To let everything come crashing in. He'll keep the secret, keep everything stowed away. The past. Himself.

Grace

THE BIRDS WAKE HER: ROBINS PRACTISING THEIR SCALES, the same notes over and over again. Grace doesn't mind. She opens her eyes and gazes out the uncurtained window. Sun warms the slender arms of the maples, the early long rays of light pulling purple out of the red flowers.

Grace knows about colour. Even before taking Kaia's colour theory course, she'd worked out some of it just by watching how her morning pee turned to green in the Tidy-Bowl blue toilet. How when she coloured maps in school, the blue of Lake Superior turned green when Ontario's yellow spilled over its coast. How the yellow grasses on the riverbank glowed orange as the red sun sank. And now she knows that when the green cedars throb purple in that same slanting end-of-day light, it must be because of the blue that green and purple share.

Grace was seventeen when she first met Kaia at a sculpture class she took one night a week. She had already been making things for many years, so was naturally drawn to sculpture. As a child, she'd watched what the crows and robins carried in their beaks in spring: long strands of straw-like grass, clumps of muddy thatch. She wove clumsy nests and perched them in trees, hoping birds would use them. After seeing an osprey nest—a massive structure of large sticks—she built one of those, loved the size of it. She made a beaver lodge, too, but that was less of a success. The imitation paper wasp nest didn't turn out so well either, but she liked the process of making paper.

Gradually, despite her mother's complaints, their yard had become her gallery, although that's not how Grace thought of it. She was just doing what she liked to do.

Grace was the youngest student in Kaia's sculpture class. The six others, several of whom were retired, had taken various art classes in the past. Grey-haired Arthur talked incessantly about the muse and about art's higher purpose. Funny that someone named Arthur talked about this. "Let's do art for Art's sake," Grace called out merrily. "Eh, Art?" As she guffawed, Arthur unclenched his teeth just enough to assert, "It's *Arthur*."

Most of the students regarded Grace with perplexity and chagrin, as if they found it irksome that someone in their art class could be so…uncultured, frankly. So unabashedly silly.

At the first class, Kaia told the students to get a feel for the medium, which was clay. Play with it, she said; work it, shape it this way and that. Stretch it, bunch it, make small pebbles with it. Pebbles. An interesting idea. Grace built a small pebble figure standing on one leg, the other leg stretched out behind, the arms outstretched as well. But the airborne arms and leg wouldn't stay in place; pieces of them kept dropping off, and she ended with a pile of rubble at the base of a partial figure. That was okay, though—letting gravity have its way. Something about impermanence, the human form being subject to laws of physics. She liked the way some of the pebbles hung on longer than others: the slow disintegration of a figure trying unsuccessfully to soar or dance. Kaia explained to Grace the use of armature in sculpture, but when Grace told her why she liked the results of her effort, Kaia understood. She invited Grace over to her house to see the fibreglass sculptures she'd been making.

Over the past few years, as their friendship has developed, Grace has been learning more about art, and Kaia has been hearing more about amphibians, insects, and a variety of other things.

"What's the story with that tree you were talking about?" Kaia asks. She and her partner, Eric, have come over to help Grace with her latest project.

"It's just a tree I found out back, uprooted. I want to put it in the front yard."

Kaia looks doubtful. "But if it's uprooted, will it transplant? Will it survive?"

"No, not like that. I'm not planning to *plant* it. Well, I am, but upside down."

"Upside down?" Eric and Kaia ask in unison.

"Roots up. You'll see. When you see it, you'll know what I mean. The roots are like hair but with stones in them. It's all wrong somehow, but that's what I want, the roots and stones in the air. You know. You'll know when you see it, once we're done with it."

Grace found the toppled spruce in the bush behind the house. She squatted down to examine the torn ground, inhaled the damp mineral smell of humus. Cobble-sized rocks were wedged into the tangle of roots still snaking from the tree trunk. When it was standing, it must have felt as if it had stones in its shoes. Looking at the roots, she felt a combination of relief and sadness. That's when she decided what she wanted to do with it.

Margaret

THE KITCHEN, DARKNESS AT THE WINDOW. MARGARET at the table doing homework, her father slouched in a chair adjacent to her, one arm draped over the chair back, a droopy smirk on his face.

"*What* kind of tree?" The peaty smell of his breath.

"A family tree, it's a project I'm supposed to do. We're all the branches of the tree. I start with me at the bottom and go backwards far as possible, who my parents are, my grandparents. So I need to know their names, when they were born and died."

His eyes sweep the room and finally focus on hers. No smirk now. "Why does your teacher need to know *that*?"

Margaret studies the page in front of her, so far with three names on it. Her mouth is dry. "It's a project. Everybody's doing one. It's about history."

He inhales through his nose. "Hmph. History." He glares at the fridge a long while. Then the half smirk again. "Lazarus." He turns his eyes on Margaret. "Put that down, then," his voice hard as iron.

Margaret squints at him, unsure. "Lazarus? He was your father?" She picks up her pencil. "Lazarus White?"

He leans forward, mimicking her. "Lazarus White?" The snarled smile straightens into a thin, tight line. Margaret lowers her eyes, heat searing her neck and face. She wants a drink of water. He leans back, shrugs a laugh. "Lazarus," he says under his breath.

Margaret shifts in her seat. Unable to talk. He glances at her. "How old are you now?"

"Eleven." Her jaw twitching. She wills it to stop.

"Eleven." He shakes his head. Takes a deep breath, exhales. "Was I eleven…?" he asks the ceiling weakly. His head droops. After a minute he says, slowly and evenly, "Edward White." Looks up at her. "My father's name was Edward Vincent White." Then he leaves the table, grabs the keys from the shelf, and walks out the door.

Florence
Humphries

THE HUMPHRIES HAD BEEN LIVING NEXT DOOR FOR YEARS, but there hadn't been much interaction between them and Grace's parents, other than a few comments about the weather. Florence and Bill had bird feeders all over their yard, and they'd sit on lawn chairs for hours, it seemed, watching the birds. It was just as if they were sitting in front of the television, but with binoculars.

But after Grace's father died, Mrs. Humphries came over and knocked on the door. She was a small woman, short and slight, a fair bit of grey in her straight dark hair, which she wore unusually long for someone her age, parted in the middle and tucked behind her ears or tied in a ponytail. She didn't have a plate of food—no casserole or meatloaf. Standing there with her hands behind her back, looking determined, she dipped her head in a curt hello.

"Florence Humphries, from next door."

Grace's mother nodded.

"We haven't been great neighbours; we're the types to keep to ourselves, Bill and I. But we want you to know if there's anything we can do for you, we're there."

Grace's mother nodded again.

"I'm not much of one for tea and chit-chat, so I don't know about dropping in on you, that kind of thing. Frankly, I don't know what to do or say. But I wanted to do this at least—come over and tell you truly and honestly that we are ready to help in any way we can."

And they did help. They put out the garbage and shovelled the driveway and sidewalks—not just Bill, but Florence too; that was one of the funny things about her. Close to fifty years old, but she didn't act like most women that age in that town.

Not long before Grace was born, Florence appeared at the door again. "What about baby clothes? My niece has a box full of clothes her baby's outgrown, and she wants to get rid of them. All in good shape. Better to you than to the dump, I say." And she smiled. She had a smile that broke her serious face wide open.

When Grace was an infant, Florence came around fairly often, her smile more in evidence. "Such a glorious spring day! Can I take the baby for a walk in the buggy? Give you some time to yourself? Nothing like a walk in the spring, wearing shoes instead of boots for the first time in months—the feet always feel so light in spring! And pushing a buggy, well that would put even more spring in my step."

She came into the house to wait while Grace was dressed for the outing. "The problem with not having children is not getting to be a grandmother—should have thought of that ten or twenty years ago! But taking little Grace for a walk, I'll feel like a temporary granny at least." She seemed quite at ease with the baby. "I've hoisted a few of these over the years," she said as she tucked Grace into the carriage. "Lots of nieces and nephews. A favourable arrangement: have fun with them and then send them home. No night feedings, no interminable exhaustion."

So when Grace was a year old and her mother started working in the housekeeping department at the hospital, it was a natural thing for Florence to start babysitting. That arrangement continued after Grace began school; she'd go to the Humphries' house afterward. When her mother arrived from work, she'd often find Florence and Grace involved in an activity she herself would never have conceived of. They'd be on their hands and knees observing something or other; once it was the number of different types of grass and other plants growing in the lawn. "Five!" shouted Grace when her mother approached. "We're up to five different species!" Another time they were lying on the grass with their ears to the ground. "Shhh," Grace whispered. "We're listening for worms." After another minute, she sat up and exclaimed, "How do those robins do it?"

After Grace's mother had been inside the Humphries' house, she understood how Florence could spend so much time bird watching or gardening, or going off to her naturalist meetings and Little Theatre rehearsals. She had time for all that because she apparently did little, if any, housework. The kitchen table was piled with magazines and books. A small box of seed packets perched on the edge of the counter amid papers and pens, a tape measure and a trowel. The rest of the counter was covered with dishes.

When the Humphries had them over for a Christmas visit, Florence had to lift a pile of newspapers off a chair so Grace's mother could sit down. She put the papers on the coffee table, which was already cluttered with a collection of rocks, several piles of magazines, and a few pairs of pants folded beneath a plastic bag containing spools of thread. Then she had to move the newspapers to the floor beneath the table to make room for a plate of store-bought Christmas cookies. Bill Humphries seemed as blind to the chaos as his wife, cheerfully pushing aside a heap of gift boxes and used wrapping paper to make room for himself on the couch.

"Don't mind the clutter," instructed Florence. "It's just what happens. You can't keep the grass from growing, or the trees from putting out leaves and seeds, or our skin cells from sloughing off, contributing to all these dust balls. Everything yearns to grow and multiply—even inanimate things like newspapers, as it turns out." She lifted a roll of chicken wire off another chair. "We need a moose for the Skits from the North Country at the Little Theatre," she explained, "so I'm going to make a moose head out of papier mache."

Florence's interest in theatre meant Grace was introduced to puppet shows, dress-up games, and improvisational dramas. The papier mache moose head was eventually joined by the heads of a caribou, a giraffe, an emu, and a toucan, as the two of them roamed in their imaginations from the tundra of northern Canada to the savannahs of Africa, the Australian outback, and the Amazon rainforest.

Margaret

BY GRADE EIGHT, THE GAP BETWEEN MARGARET and some of the girls—the bolder ones, especially—is quite large. Her classmates have known for years that Margaret and another girl, Sally Duncan, are "holy rollers," but as they all move toward adolescence, this fact matters more. It's partly because of the way Margaret dresses. While mini skirts are dawning, she wears drab below-the-knee dresses sewn by her mother.

Margaret doesn't feel welcome hanging around with the larger gang of girls who lean against the back wall of the school: the territory presided over by Vanessa and her pack. But the stories of Vanessa's exploits trickle through the entire social strata. Her two older brothers have taken her to their parties and introduced her to marijuana, booze, and older guys. At least that's what Vanessa brags about when her hangers-on gather round her at recess.

One day, Vanessa wears a skirt so short she gets sent home from school. "Serves her right," clucks Sally in the washroom at recess, as the other girls gush over Vanessa's audacity. "Coming to school dressed like that, with sin written all over her." The dead silence following Sally's comment makes Margaret wince. She busies herself at the sink, washing her hands. The girls suddenly disperse, leaving Sally and Margaret alone in the washroom.

"They're all just as bad as Vanessa," huffs Sally. Margaret doesn't respond. She dries her hands and walks out into the schoolyard, not sure how to pass the excruciating eleven minutes remaining in the break.

There's a dream Margaret often has, growing up. She's in a public washroom: drab walls, metal echoes, murky pool of fluorescent lighting. Trying to wipe shit off herself. No matter how much she wipes, she can't get it all off, there's always more, and more, and more, and the more she wipes, the more broadly it gets smeared on her body. It seems to go on forever, this dream, and the stain of it lingers long after she wakes.

Margaret comes home from school one day with a small, glossy booklet the nurse gave her. She finds her mother cleaning her parents' bedroom and mentions the pamphlet, as the nurse instructed. Her mother takes it, frowns at the cover, and opens it to a diagram of the female reproductive system. "So they teach you that in school now. What other filth do they teach?"

"It was just the nurse, in her office. The girls were going in one at a time. She asked if I knew about menestration, and gave me the booklet to bring home."

Her mother clears her throat. "Fine then." She puts the pamphlet down. "When you start bleeding, you'll need these." She opens the closet door, pulls a box of Kotex from a corner of the closet. "I'll put some in your room."

She puts the box back, closes the door, stands for several seconds with her back to Margaret. Then she turns and says, "When the bleeding starts, it's a warning about staying pure." She pauses. "You should pray for guidance…pray to the Lord to help keep you pure, in your thoughts and actions."

When Margaret gets her first period, she dreams she is swimming in a glassy blue lake. She's naked, the water satin against her skin. She feels so clean. As she swims, a river of blood begins to stream out behind her. It keeps flowing out of her until the lake itself turns red. She's swimming in blood; red waves lap against the shore, staining the sand and the rocks and shells. People are gathering on the shore, taunting, angry, telling her to get out of the water. But she can't because she's naked. Suddenly the scene changes and there's a cave at the edge of the water. She swims into the cave, clambers onto the rocks inside. It's a broad and silent cavern echoing water sounds. She reaches between her legs and then with bloody fingers paints her name across the granite wall: Margaret Eleanor White.

Grace

THE HUMPHRIES WERE NATURALISTS, people knowledgeable about nature—which was not the same as the people who like to go around without clothes on, Mrs. Humphries once explained with a laugh. They both knew a lot, especially about birds. They explained that some adult birds partially digested their food, and when they got back to the nest, they'd regurgitate it for the young birds to eat if the babies pecked a certain spot on the parent's face. How did the baby birds know to peck that particular spot? Why couldn't the mother just throw up the food on her own? Maybe the mother didn't really want to, but the babies would find a way to make it happen, force the mother to feed them.

Other girls Grace's age weren't much interested in that type of thing. She tried playing with them but wasn't very good at it. Tina Parker had a little pink plastic pony with a long, iridescent purple mane. The colour was great, but all that girl did with this pony, over and over, was comb its mane. She said it was a magical pony, but she couldn't even explain what kinds of magical things it could do. "It can fly," offered Tina, in response to Grace's question. "See?" She held the pony aloft and waved her arm around.

"If it's magic, maybe it could turn itself into something else, like a dinosaur or something—how 'bout while it's flying, it turns into a purple pterodactyl?!"

With a *humph*, Tina clutched the pony to her chest with two hands, turned on her heel, and marched away, her ponytail swinging like a pendulum.

Before long, the girls began to ignore Grace, forming tight circles with their backs to her when they saw her coming. Eventually a chant accompanied this action: *Grace, Grace, from outer space.* Their little circle like a planetary mass, Grace became their moon, and orbited them a few times before spinning off on her own again.

Grace has never been very interested in outer space. She wouldn't mind seeing Earth from space, the way astronauts can, that blue-green globe partially illuminated by the sun. But otherwise she wouldn't want to spend time out there, because nothing could quite compare to this planet with its indigo lakes and turquoise oceans, its blue-sky atmosphere, its life. Standing outside on a late September morning and inhaling autumn smells—you wouldn't get those on Mars. Or the sight of starlings flying across the yard in a loose flock, and then as they approach a tree, they get sucked up into the branches in one big swoop, as if there was a vacuum cleaner in the tree. Or the sound of caterpillars chewing; that's an amazing thing. When there's an outbreak of tent caterpillars eating up the leaves on the trees, you can stand underneath and actually hear them chewing.

All these small things add up to something big—so big her chest aches, as if thinking about them is something she does with her heart instead of her brain.

But isn't that part of the heart's job, not just to circulate blood but to translate the messages received by our senses? Otherwise, how would we know what anything means?

Margaret

AT SUPPER ONE NIGHT, AFTER DRAINING ANOTHER beer, Margaret's father sits back in his chair. Her mother's face is pinched; she's managed to ignore his belch during grace and has been focussing on the business of cutting her pork chop into miniscule pieces and chewing each one to smithereens.

"Saw old Frank Baxter the other night," says Hal. "Your friend's husband."

Iris stops chewing momentarily. Her eyes dart toward Hal and then back to her plate.

"At the Legion. He had us in stitches. Could hardly walk, he was so hammered."

Iris inhales sharply, exhales slowly. Clears her throat.

"Grabbing the waitress's ass like he hadn't had any for ages."

"Enough."

"But he'll be at church with the Mrs. on Sunday, I'm sure."

A screaming silence. Margaret can't look at either of them. From the corner of her eye, she sees the jerk of her mother's arm. The plate nails her father in the chest. Margaret is frozen in her seat.

Her father, after the initial jolt, pulls the mashed potatoes off his shirt, pauses a second as he stares at the pale glob of it in his hand. Stands up calmly and walks toward the sink. When he gets behind his wife's chair, he suddenly reaches around, grabs her chin with his free hand and stuffs the mess of potatoes into her face. She tries to jerk her head free but he keeps pushing the potatoes into her nose and mouth.

Margaret stares across the table, her knife and fork still poised above her plate. Finally her mother yanks his hands away and stumbles out of the chair. Her father shakes the remaining bits of potato from his hand and disappears into the bathroom.

Her mother is at the kitchen sink, cleaning potatoes from her face. Margaret slides quietly out of her seat. She picks off the floor small chunks of pork, round slices of carrots, flecks of mashed potato, and discards them. Then she stands there, not sure what to say.

Grace

GRACE'S MOTHER WAS NEVER MUCH OF A TALKER. As a child, Grace made up for her mother's silence, as if there was an equilibrium she was responsible for maintaining. At the supper table, she'd tell her mother about all the things she'd done in a day, the things she'd seen and learned. A fly getting caught in a spider web, how the spider wrapped its silk around the snagged and madly buzzing fly and then sucked its insides out. How crows are so playful they will slide down snowbanks—they slide down and then fly back up to the top and slide down again, just like tobogganing. How the seed pods of jewel weed have a fine spring mechanism that causes them to go SPROING when you touch them—it feels like a tiny explosion between your fingers when they spring open and the seeds fly out. Her mother would look up from her food periodically and study Grace for a minute as if she was trying to sort out whether the child across from her was someone she knew. Once, in response to this expression, Grace stopped in the middle of an explanation about a salamander's ability to regrow severed limbs, and peered at her mother. "It's Grace," she said.

Her mother blinked several times and nodded.

Margaret

IT'S NOT HER IDEA, REALLY, TO BE PLUNGED into the water and rise up out of it spluttering, as she's seen several people do over the years that her mother's been bringing her to the immersions. Now that she's getting older, closer to adulthood, her mother's been promoting the idea. Margaret knows it's supposed to be the Lord calling you, not just your mother pushing you. But Margaret's mother is persuasive, if not in the logic of her arguments, at least in the persistence with which she presents them. Her mother seems to think that, now that the baptismal dress is sewn, the Lord will surely call, as if responding to a white flag of surrender.

It's cool for July, the sky weighted down with imminent rain. They're in the municipal park, mowed grass ending in a narrow strip of sand and rocks at the water's edge. The river that winds through the town is about fifty metres wide, and normally by July its flow is considerably reduced. But this year there's been so much rain that it's running high and fast, even here at the summertime swimming area.

The congregants huddle in their summer coats in a semicircle behind the three people dressed in white who stand at the river's edge. Russ Caple, the only adult among the three, wades out to meet Pastor Wilkins, waist-deep in the water. The pastor exclaims, *I indeed baptize you with water; but one mightier than I cometh, the latchet of whose shoes I am not worthy to unloose: he shall baptize you with the Holy Ghost and with fire.* He puts one arm behind Russ and tips him back into the river, submersing him. Russ bursts back up from the water smiling, praising God as those on shore join in with joyous halleluiahs.

Sally Duncan is next. At fourteen years old, she's short and plump, encased in a high-necked, long-sleeved white dress, the billowing skirt of which almost reaches the ground. When Pastor Wilkins beckons her, she wades into the water uncertainly. She's told Margaret that she's been praying to overcome her fear of the water. Mrs. Duncan is singing, there's a swell of prayers pushing out toward the girl from shore. She's chest-deep when she reaches Pastor Wilkins. Is it rapture in her face, or terror? The Reverend places a hand on her back, shouts the incantation, and pushes on her shoulder to tip her backwards. One of Sally's arms flies up; the pastor loses his balance. Her meagre, high-pitched voice disappears with her beneath the river's surface. Pastor Wilkins regains his footing, leans forward, his arms thrashing in the water. The river is roiling as if a million fish are nipping at insects on the surface and Reverend Wilkins is trying to catch one with his bare hands. Then he stops, scans the water all around him. Everyone on shore is holding their breath, and so is the sky, and so is God. Until Pastor Wilkins dives under, and the spell is broken. God suddenly exhales, and people scatter like dandelion seeds blown from their stem, some along the shore, some into the water, some in frantic circles, wobbly ellipses, voices like sparks swirling upward to singe the wings of gulls crying overhead.

Just downriver, something pale streams near the surface, drifting in the current like a barely submerged sail or an angel whose wings can't break through the river's grey skin.

At Sally's funeral, Pastor Wilkins' impassioned words barely register with Margaret. They swim in and out of her consciousness.

... a blessing... taken home to the Lord...

Margaret pictures Sally's mother on the shore, screaming and falling to the ground, a flock of women settling around her, flutters and murmurs followed by stillness. Then her cries rising up again, and more flapping along with them, until the group settles once more.

... baptized not just with water but with the spirit, filled with the breath of salvation...

And downstream a group of men closing around a white bundle on the grass, working on it, trying to push the baptismal water and the breath of salvation out of Sally's lungs and fill them with oxygen instead. Margaret remembers watching all of this from inside a bubble, the sounds around her growing more and more distant as she stood on the sand, unable to move—almost like the dream she's had since then, drifting in an underwater silence, her hair a wavering halo round her head, the only sound a muffled drum, her heartbeat thick and slow, her own white dress tugging her down and down.

She's pulled back to the present, Pastor Wilkins saying that Sally is with God this moment. She looks at the people around her, most of them nodding their heads and uttering praise. They weren't next in line that day, as Margaret was, waiting to be pushed beneath swirling water unlit by the sun. She tries to picture what the preacher is saying, Sally beaming in God's company. But she can't see Sally, or God. She can't see anything.

Grace

"DO I HAVE GRANDPARENTS?"

Grace's mother was startled.

"We're doing a project at school about the Depression, and I'm supposed to talk to people who were around then, like parents and grandparents."

Her mother busied herself with the dust rag. "I thought learning came from books."

"We learned some stuff about it already. It was a dust bowl and everybody was poor and men rode trains around looking for work. She gave us some questions we could ask, like how old were you during the Depression?"

"I was hardly born yet, so I don't know anything about it. All I know is nobody had much money when I was growing up."

"What about grandparents—do I have any?"

"No."

"Your parents are dead?"

A pause. "Yes."

"What about my other grandparents, my father's parents?"

"I don't know anything about them, other than they lived in a town called Drayton."

"You never met them?"

"No, never did."

Later: "I can't find Drayton on a map."

Grace's mother stared at her, expressionless.

"Drayton—you said that's where my father was from. Where is it?"

"I don't know—over by Chapleau somewhere. He said it was small. Sawmill town. Maybe it's too small for a map."

"That's where my father was born?"

"As far as I know."

"Maybe my grandparents are still alive there. Maybe I could meet them."

"Your father said his father was killed in the sawmill."

"Killed! Like, murdered?!"

"No, caught in the saw or something."

"Ugh! Killed by a saw!" Her grandfather inside a box that a magician would cut through, after which her grandfather would supposedly emerge, miraculously unscathed. But the magician's concern as it became apparent something was going wrong, the saw meeting with too much pulpy resistance, the screams from inside the box far too convincing. The magician tried to smile through gritted teeth, and continued his laborious sawing, although the audience was losing interest, especially after the screaming stopped. Eventually they all shambled out while the magician, sweating now, his mascara streaming and his top hat on the floor, continued sawing, sawing, sawing through gristle and bone, until he collapsed from exhaustion.

Of course that was not how it happened.

Margaret

HE SHOWS UP AT THE HIGH SCHOOL ONE DAY, a couple weeks into the school year. Pale and skinny, dark stringy hair to his shoulders, bangs in his eyes. In Barret River, not many guys have hair that long, even in 1973.

He's in Margaret's Man-in-Society class. The room goes a bit quiet when he walks in the first time; kids stop talking momentarily as they turn their eyes toward him for a few seconds and then away. He saunters nonchalantly down an aisle and slouches into an empty desk. Margaret glances nervously over at the new guy and then toward the door. Joe Dinelli, the football star, strolls in and stops half-way down the aisle when he sees his seat is occupied. The room is getting quiet again. Joe says, "Hey, that's my desk," and the new guy looks past him and shrugs, just as Mr. Galloway begins to clear his throat and address the class.

"Okay, Dinelli, grab a seat," he says, when he notices Joe standing in the aisle.

Joe turns toward the teacher. "My seat's already been grabbed, Mr. G."

"Well grab another one then."

Joe scowls but takes an empty desk close to the front.

The next day, Joe is already in his usual seat when the new guy arrives. He scans the room casually as he enters. Without expression he takes the empty desk across the aisle from Margaret, who sits in the far corner.

Margaret is sixteen. With her babysitting money she's been buying her own clothes. But she has already become a social outcast, especially in the eyes of the "in" crowd, the clique of jocks and their girlfriends and cheerleaders, whom Margaret regards with a combination of disdain and envy.

She eats lunch with Nancy Lee and Earla Franks. Nancy is small and quiet; Earla large and loud. She has to eat lunch with *some*body. Everyone has a regular spot in the cafeteria; theirs is the back corner.

David Lockwood, the new kid, is also drawn to corners, and there are several empty chairs at Margaret's lunch table. David begins sitting there too, apart from the three girls, but at the same table. He always has a book, and chews as he reads.

When Margaret sees how he can be so easily alone with a book, she becomes interested in reading—at least in the idea of reading. She has been utterly floored by the English teacher's expectation that students would actually read entire books—novels like *Fahrenheit 451* and *The Chrysalids*.

In Man-in-Society class, the teacher is fond of group discussions and pairs work, which Margaret hates. Because David is now sitting across from her, they end up in groups together. The first time, their task is to examine a diagram and come up with some ideas about what the diagram depicts—what this thing could be, and what it might be used for. The diagram shows a collection of rectangles arranged in a circle. There are pairs of vertical rectangles, and each pair is bridged by a horizontal rectangle across the top. David knows right away that it is Stonehenge.

"A stone hedge?" says Earla, dubiously.

"Stone*henge*," replies David. "It's in England, an ancient astronomy thing."

Margaret and Earla look at each other and then back at David, who is studying the diagram.

"They're huge stones, quarried and cut somehow, and placed just so. At sunrise on the summer solstice, the sun comes through between two of these stones and shines on a certain spot."

"What's summer solsys?" asks Earla.

"June 21, longest day of the year. First day of summer."

Margaret ventures a question. "How do you know about this Stonehenge?"

"Read about it. Some people think it has to do with Druids, that it was a place where they'd have ceremonies."

"What's a Druid?" Margaret is glad Earla has no modesty about asking questions that betray her general ignorance.

"Priests. Celtic priests, from old pagan days. They'd have fertility rites; their religion was all connected to the seasons, the earth, fertility."

"So they'd want to know about the official start of summer." Earla again.

"I guess they were tracking things, the cycles. Whoever made Stonehenge knew about the cyclic nature of the sun's movements. They had a precise enough knowledge to build this thing so that the light would come through to that particular spot on the solstice." He pauses. "Then they probably started partying their fucking brains out," he says, and grins.

"Where do you read about this stuff?" Margaret wants to know.

He shrugs. "*National Geographic*. Books."

Earla rolls her eyes. "Boring."

At lunch one day, Margaret leans across the two empty chairs next to her and asks David what he's reading.

He holds up the book. "Hermann Hesse. *Narcissus and Goldmund*."

Margaret squints at the book, unable to distinguish between the author's name and the title. A bunch of odd-sounding names. She wants to have some kind of conversation, but can't think of what to say next.

David observes her perplexity. "I like Hesse—have read a few of his books. He's kind of philosophical."

"Oh yeah?" asks Margaret weakly. "Like how?"

David frowns. "About life. You know—the meaning of life and all that." He flips through the book, finds a dog-eared page. "Like here, Narcissus is talking about wanting to serve only the spirit within him, as he understands its commands, rather than serving something else. You know, like serving a church or a government or even public opinion—that kind of idea."

"Huh. Cool." The spirit within, thinks Margaret. Someone writes that kind of thing in a book without calling it the Holy Spirit, like at church. "Is that *your* book?"

He seems puzzled by the question. "Yeah." Then he chuckles. "Good thing I guess, since I've marked it all up. That's the thing about Hesse; I'm always underlining lines I like. It's not just a regular novel or story. You read something and then you look around and you say, Yeah, he's got *that* right."

"Could I see your book?" Margaret feels as though she has just leapt off a tall building.

David shrugs and hands it across to her, watches her flip through it. The print is small, just what she hates in a book. Small print always makes her fall asleep. But many pages are bent over in the corner with passages underlined. She reads one underlined part, about how life is hard to understand, how nobody really knows anything. Which is exactly how she feels: not knowing anything. She wants to be able to say something nonchalantly clever, but her awareness of David watching her, waiting for a reaction, and the heat searing her neck and face muddle her concentration. "Could I borrow it sometime, when you're done reading it?" she asks in what sounds to her like a strained squeak.

"Yeah, sure," he says, taking the book back. "You like reading?"

"Um, well, kind of. I don't really read much, so far. Stuff for school…."

Vagueness is no refuge for Margaret. She feels hopelessly exposed.

David rolls his eyes. "The school stuff is shit. *Moonfleet* and all that. They want to feed us pablum so we don't really start thinking—that would be too dangerous."

David isn't afraid to sound smart; he doesn't seem to care about what the "in" crowd thinks of him. He's cool in a way the cool kids are not: they act and move self-consciously, as if on a stage, knowing people are watching them and admiring their special grace, their ease, their unbearable confidence. David ambles through the halls and aisles as if he's the only person on earth, and as if it's actually interesting being the planet's sole inhabitant. He appears indifferent to the social hierarchy—or even better, disdainful of it.

One lunchtime the cheerleaders make an appearance in the cafeteria, shaking their pom-poms as they strut down the aisles brightly uttering school cheers in preparation for an important football game. David slouches deeper into his seat and mutters, "Bunch of sheep," as he lifts his book in front of his face.

"Sheep?"

"Dumb animals that follow each other around because they can't fucking think for themselves."

Earla scowls at him. "They're just showing school spirit, nothing wrong with that."

It surprises Margaret, the delight that tumbles out of her mouth in a laugh. "Sheep!" she cries, ignoring Earla's disapproving frown. "It's true!" David looks up with a smirk, then turns back to his book.

Margaret feels as though some of the straightjacket's buckles have just given way: a couple up around her chest. It is interesting to breathe.

Margaret runs into David one day in front of the Peacock Garden restaurant.

"What's up?" he asks.

"Nothing much, just shopping a bit."

"Shopping."

"Well, looking around, clothes and things. What are you doing?"

"Hanging out. Going in for a coffee; want to come?"

"Sure," she says, wishing she felt sure, both excited by and terrified of the prospect of making conversation over coffee.

On one side of the restaurant, a counter with stools runs the length of the room, and on the other side are booths with iridescent vinyl seat covers: peacock blue. Margaret follows David to a booth, hesitating before sliding in across from him, not sure whether she should sit on the same side as David or on the opposite side. She has never been in a restaurant before.

She scans the décor. "Chinese," she says.

"What was your first clue?"

"I've never been in here."

"Where do you hang out?"

"Nowhere really. I don't go out much."

"How come?"

She shrugs. "You come here a lot?"

"Yeah, I come in for coffee, bring a book. It's my main hangout. Nobody from school comes here; I like that about it. Mainly rubbies and other real people come in here, especially late at night."

"You come here late at night?"

"Sure, why not? Where else would I go? I'm not into the school things—dances, basketball games, all that crap. You?"

"No. My mother doesn't want me going to dances anyway."

"No big loss. But is she old-fashioned or something?"

"Yeah. Religious." She grimaces. "Dancing's a sin."

He rolls his eyes. "Oh, one of those."

"Yeah, one of those."

"What else is a sin? Must be lots of things that are sins in her book."

"Just about everything, in my mother's eyes, is wrong, wrong, wrong."

"What religion—she a Baptist or something?"

"Pentecostal."

"So, no dancing, no drinking, no screwing, no card games—what else?"

"No movies. Do nothing on Sunday, no work or any kind of exercise like biking or swimming."

He shakes his head. "You go along with all that?"

Margaret frowns. "Hard not to, with *my* mother. Bad enough now I buy my own clothes. She always sewed them all, but I won't wear them any more. That's been a big fight."

"Man. How do you stand it?"

"I don't know. Might be easier if I had brothers or sisters."

"Only child? Me too."

"What are your parents like? Not religious?"

"No. They think my hair's too long, I sleep too much, all that. But they're all right. They like that I read a lot. We talk about stuff—books, politics, what's happening. They're pretty cool overall."

Margaret can't imagine this. "I wish I had parents like yours."

"So why worry about what yours think? Just do what you want to do."

"Yeah, right."

"Tomorrow's Sunday. Let's get together and play cards over a few drinks." He grins.

She hesitates, wanting to take him seriously but not sure if he's joking. "Maybe after church," she says, and they both laugh. The laughter a gauge: so far, so good.

"Maybe I'll come by and pick you up just before church; that oughta give your mother something to pray about."

"She'd kill me. After she finished killing you."

"Sounds like a challenge I can't resist. Where do you live?"

Margaret looks down at the cup between her hands. It's the first time she's drunk coffee. The first time she's had a conversation like this. She's nervous and exhilarated at the same time, her stomach tight with worry she'll ruin everything by saying or doing the wrong thing. Is he serious? Should she answer?

"We go to Calvary Pentecostal for the 11 a.m. service, usually arriving at quarter to. You could kidnap me from the parking lot." Humour is a good dodge, and she's astonished to find herself using it.

"You don't still go to church with her, do you?"

Margaret slouches back against the booth. "Well… It's easier than fighting about it."

The next morning at 10:45, as Margaret and her mother approach the church entrance, David calls her name and saunters over.

Her mother stiffens. "Who on earth—?" She scowls at Margaret. "Keep moving."

But he's already in front of them. "Hey, Margaret—ready to go?"

Margaret and her mother both stare at him.

"Come on, let's split." He nods at the older woman, takes Margaret by the arm, and turns her toward the road.

"Margaret, get back here. We are going into the church."

Margaret is too stunned to answer. She lets her feet travel in the direction David is steering her.

"Margaret White, you listen to me."

David is trying not to let Margaret's hesitation impede their progress. "She does seem rather severe," he chuckles.

Margaret looks sideways at him and then away, and then back toward the church where her mother is still glaring at them. Even after they've rounded the corner, she keeps turning and looking in the direction of the church.

"You told me to kidnap you. Seemed too good a scene to miss."

"You don't have to live with her after."

"What about your old man—he doesn't go to church with you?"

"No."

"How does he get away with it if you can't?"

There is no way to answer this question. "I can't believe we did this." Margaret is shaking all over, arms crossed, starting to laugh. "Oh my god, I can't believe it."

"Okay, so that was step one. Step two, a little Sunday toke. Come on, we'll head down to the river."

Margaret doesn't know how she let this happen. David is watching her as he pulls a lumpy cigarette out of his shirt pocket.

"Ever seen a joint before?"

She clamps her jaw shut but can't stop her face from twitching. Shakes her head. Too late now to get out of this.

He explains how to smoke it, demonstrating with the first toke. He's holding his breath as he hands her the joint. She almost drops it and he laughs.

"Just hold it between your thumb and finger—there. Don't inhale big, just take it slow."

He laughs again as she coughs, then takes the joint from her. "That always happens at first. You'll get the hang of it."

After they finish the joint, they walk along the trail that follows the river. David is quiet, chuckling every now and then. Margaret feels no influence from the dope and is wondering why she's here, how she got into this, how she will face her mother when she gets home. Wondering what's happening with this boy who has befriended her. He's just ahead of her on the trail, moving through sunlight that's scissoring through the trees.

At the edge of a small open area, he stops and looks up through the branches of a giant white pine. "What a great perspective. Gotta contemplate that awhile, come on." He lies down on the yellowed pine needles littering the ground and gazes up through the canopy. "Have a look," he says to Margaret. She tilts her head back. "Easier on the ground," he says.

She looks behind her and around, inspecting the area with feigned interest. Stalling. Finally she perches on a stump a short distance from David, pinning her knees together and straightening her skirt. She's miserable, she misses her normal life. The rough stump jabs and numbs. Margaret removes her jacket and arranges it on the ground so she can sit on it and lean against the stump. It takes awhile to hear the silence in the background, so loud is the noise inside her, a buzzing that begins in her stomach and spreads through her chest and into her head. She gazes up through the pine at the puzzle of blue sky, the varying shades of green in the tree's fine needles, some of which appear lit from within.

She and David are quiet for a long while. The dry-earth smell of the bush in autumn: dead leaves and needles warmed by the sun. Her stomach relaxes.

"Feel so small here beside this tree," she says.

"It's like looking through binoculars backwards," he says—"you know that long, telescoping view, so everything seems so far away."

Margaret has never used binoculars. "The sky is far away but close at the same time."

"Maybe this is like the Bodhi tree."

"The what?"

"The tree the Buddha sat under when he reached nirvana."

"Nervanna?"

"Enlightenment. Don't you know about the Buddha?"

"I'm a Pentecostal, remember?"

"Oh, right." Then he's laughing, in a desultory way. "The look on your mother's face."

Margaret is quiet. She doesn't want to think about her mother.

"How do you stand it? Living with her."

Margaret has no answer.

"What about your dad, what's he like?"

"I don't see him much. He's out late a lot."

"Out late. Working?"

She hesitates. "I don't know. Drinking."

"I bet your mother likes that."

"They fight a lot."

"Fight, like how?"

"Argue. Throw things."

"That's really Christian."

Margaret doesn't answer.

"What do you do, when they're fighting?"

"Stay in my room."

He rolls onto his side to face her. "Pretty fucked-up scene."

She closes her eyes. Swallows hard.

"So maybe we should do this every Sunday, smoke drugs and sit under the Bodhi tree. Change your religion."

≈

It's David who nicknames her Maggie.

"*Margaret.* It sounds like a grandmother's name. How about Maggie? Like in the Rod Stewart song."

"Rod Stewart?"

"Oh, God." He sighs. "Life with a Pentecostal. I've taught you to smoke pot and French kiss, and now I have to introduce you to good music too."

Margaret shrinks a bit.

"In the song, Stewart is telling the girl—Maggie—to wake up." David leers at her. "See, the guy in the song is sleeping with Maggie." She tries not to blush, has no response. Her sense of humour often fails her at key moments. "I suppose I could teach you that, too," he says, grinning, and puts his arms around her.

She pushes him away. "I'm not fully converted to your religion yet," she says, trying to find firm ground, a comfortable place to respond from.

"Speaking of my religion—though I don't really have one—have you finished reading *Siddhartha* yet?"

She's about to be found out. "Not yet ..."

"How far in are you?"

"Um, well, not very far."

"You're not into it." He's disappointed.

"I don't know. It's kind of slow and wordy."

"That's Hesse, man. It's not a fucking Harlequin romance."

She tries a slight change of subject. "We have that book report coming up for Galloway's class. I don't know any of those books on the list."

"*Catcher in the Rye*," he says. "You've gotta read *Catcher in the Rye*."

"Catch Her in the Rye. Sounds like my father; he likes the rye."

"You'll like this book. I'll lend you my copy."

"Did you underline half of every page in that one too? That makes it hard to read."

"Get your own copy then if you don't like my underlining."

"What's it about?"

"A guy in prep school, a social outcast. He's got problems, but he sees the hypocrisy everywhere. He knows what's going on, calls it like it is."

Maggie picks up the small paperback, a plain red cover with the title and Salinger's name written in yellow on the front and back. She opens it. Ugh. There are hardly any margins; the pages are crammed with small print. But she begins reading, and soon enough is drawn in by the guy telling the story. Someone her age, with a lousy childhood, who doesn't fit in with the cool crowd and is a bit of a loner. If he was a girl, she'd be hooked. As it is, she finds herself wading through some parts, though overall she's amazed this book exists: someone speaking to her from a life that has some parallels to hers. Holden's loneliness. His awkwardness—though he is far more confident than she is. The way he hates phonies. It's the first time she's read anything that sounded familiar to her, the first time she's encountered a recognizable character, someone who, at times, speaks her own thoughts and reflects her own feelings.

"Have you read the Salinger book yet?" asks David. They're having coffee at the Peacock Garden. Andy, the owner, is standing on a chair in the corner behind David. He's removing from the ceiling a strip of fly paper studded black with houseflies.

"Yeah. I just finished it."

"Well? What did you think?"

She watches Andy hang a brand new strip of fly paper. "It's good."

"That's all? *It's good?*"

She shifts forward on the bench seat, grasps the coffee cup with both hands. "That Holden guy, he's...."

David is waiting.

She takes a breath, decides to let the words just tumble out. "He's funny, but sad too. I like the way he talks about all the phonies."

David chuckles. "He's got good antenna for phoniness, that's for sure. I love the way he describes those rich old bastards at the school—old Ossenburger the undertaker, all that. He nails everybody right on."

"Yeah."

"He tries to be such a big shot but it doesn't work—he's mostly so pathetic—and yet he's smarter than just about everybody else."

"He's lonely," she says. "He talks like he's okay, but really he's lonely. He doesn't belong anywhere."

"He's hilarious, though. I love the way he talks, so sardonic."

"Yeah," says Maggie, wondering what sardonic means.

"And the bit about hitching out west and pretending he's a deaf mute so he doesn't have to talk to anybody—even his wife would have to write notes to him like everybody else. That's a riot."

They're startled by the sound of dishes crashing to the floor in the kitchen, followed by Andy's high-pitched yelling.

"I liked his sister, Phoebe," Maggie ventures.

"She was okay. What's interesting is he wanted to be the catcher in the rye, but really it was Phoebe who caught him."

"It's good he had her for a sister. I wish I had a sister like that."

"So have you started the book report yet? It's due in a couple days."

"I know; I've got to get started on it." She bats a fly away from her cup, watches it circle up and around and then land smack in the middle of the sticky orange strip hanging in the corner. "I never know what to say."

"Simple. Read the sheet Galloway handed out and follow the instructions."

"Simple for you." She watches the trapped fly. It buzzes madly for a bit, and then is still.

In the winter, the trail along the river is deep with snow, so they walk out along a road at the edge of town that dead-ends where a snowmobile trail begins. Sometimes they walk along that trail awhile. They smoke pot on the walk and then return to David's house to hang out in the basement rec room, where they listen to music and make out. His parents respect their privacy, but Maggie feels safe there. She knows David can't interpret her resistance to his gropings as mere prudishness: one of his parents could walk in on them any time.

One Saturday, David takes Maggie over to Benny Lutz's place. She's nervous because she knows Benny sells pot, and she's picturing a seedy lair about to be raided by the cops any minute. Even though she's wearing the coolest clothes she owns, her Levi jeans and a paisley blouse, she feels like Little Miss Priss knocking on the door to distribute Biblical tracts. It turns out the house is a small rectangular bungalow just like all the others on his street; it's his parents' place and he inhabits the basement. His parents are out, though; the table in his room is thick with weed he's bagging up, and the three of them are free to smoke with Pink Floyd cranked up.

David, as always, is analyzing the lyrics. "I love that line about the lunatics in the hall—their pictures in the newspapers on the floor, every day the paperboy bringing more. All those faces on the front pages—politicians, generals, the great fucking leaders of the world." He likes to hear himself talk, with brave, grave words. Critical, questioning words. Maggie lets David's words fill her up. She swallows whole sentences, entire diatribes. And strangely enough, develops a taste for David's brand of ideas. But there's a sigh and an accompanying expression on his face sometimes, when she's talking. It's a look that says she's failing, despite her efforts to please him. So mostly she holds on to her own words the way a good poker player holds cards. She's not yet ready to abandon her watchfulness.

One day David is reading aloud Japanese poetry, not exactly haiku, but similar.

> *Adrift all night*
> *on the Bay of Sumi*
> *my small boat*
> *waits for dawn.*

Maggie wonders if she'll ever be able to speak as clearly as these brief poems do. Each one is like a small bird lighting on her open hand; she feels the weight of air in her palm, the beating of a tiny heart. But she can't find words to fit the thoughts she carries, to give them wing, launch them into the world.

≈

Another time at Benny's when his parents are away, Benny pulls out a bottle of tequila. David says it's better than other booze; it's more like a drug high, because it's made from a plant in Mexico, sort of like magic mushrooms only it's cactus or something. Normally David prefers drugs to booze because of the pyschedelic effect; it's more mind expanding, he says. But tequila's a trip too. Benny and David are amused by Maggie's response to the searing sharpness of the salt-tequila-lemon trio; to her it feels like swallowing shrapnel. With each shot, though, she grimaces less.

Then she's gone, falling away into blankness.

David's tongue, a million tongues on her neck as she arches to the surface, pressing against him. Is that her breath she hears? Benny's laugh, like someone shovelling coal. She sinks again into silence. Dreams she's in a warm sea, naked, every molecule in her skin dancing. She's riding a wave. A sumptuous wave. The water warm and soft between her legs. No, David's head? There? But she's drowning, a sound like her throat full of water, guttural. Suddenly she's being split in two, ripped up the middle. Her voice, something wordless, a howl. David's face over hers, and then his body on top of her, limp and moaning. Something else, an animal nearby being strangled. In the weak yellow light of the spinning room, she descries Benny in the armchair, legs stretched out in front of him, pants open, something inside his hand leaking milk.

David seems unconscious on top of her and she can't breathe. She rolls him off, tries to sit up. Benny's long, low laugh from the chair. "Oh baby, that was great. You guys can fuck here anytime."

He walks her almost all the way home; their usual practice. Both of them shaky from the tequila. Both quiet, continents apart. When they get to Maggie's street, he turns toward her, his eyes skimming across her forehead. "See you at school," David says, and hesitates. He puts his hand on her arm, leans in and kisses her lightly, then turns and leaves.

This is Saturday. School is Monday. Normally they meet at the river on Sunday.

Finding Grace

Maggie goes down to the river, just in case. After lingering awhile at their meeting place, she walks alone along the trail to the old pine. It was early autumn when they first sat under this tree; now, it's mid May. The river is high, rushing silently along the bank. An hour's drive from here, it empties into a lake the size of a sea. Maggie doesn't really care about that lake or the river. This pine, though, she thinks of as "theirs." Today she finds no comfort here. A harsh light pushes through bare birches and fractures on the ground. Pine needles that had coloured the earth bright apricot last fall have faded to a dull brown, like the matted clumps of damp leaves strewn along the path. A year ago she wouldn't have noticed any of these details. Hanging out with David has changed her perception—oddly enough, sharpening it. And what her senses tell her now is that everything is wrong.

The wages of sin is death. The Lord's righteous plan for her destroyed, Satan having had his way. Words like that have invaded her. She doesn't believe the words but she can't banish them. Maybe she should pray, go back to church. No, not that. She lies on her bed, raises her palms toward heaven. *Don't let me be pregnant.* She tries to remember how it happened, how she let it happen, but the picture won't hold still. The parts she does recall replay over and over, a film gone off the sprockets, images stuttering on a screen. She can't turn off the projector; it plays on and on.

At lunch on Monday, David comes into the cafeteria to buy a sandwich, but he doesn't come over to their table. Maggie sees him pay the cashier and leave without looking her way. Watches him joke with Jamie Edgars on the way out.

She dreams she's in a hospital, some kind of institution. Two white bisecting hallways, a fluorescent vibration. She's trying to find someone, maybe David, walking up and down the hallways, shading her eyes from the harsh glare of the lights. One door is open, she walks into a dimly lit room, the darkness a relief but her eyes have trouble adjusting. The room appears empty, but there's a small noise in the corner. Then someone is there, he's upon her before she can see who it is, he has a knife and he's slashing at her, he's carving up her face. A voice, is it hers as she crashes through to waking? *The blood of the lamb is shed for you.*

David does come to the lunch table on Tuesday, but later than usual. Maggie is sitting alone, forcing her eyes to move along the printed lines in a book.

"What are you reading?"

Her heart is beating too fast. She holds up the book for him to see.

"*Siddhartha.* I thought you gave up on that."

"I was at the Bodhi tree on Sunday."

He looks away, coughs. Eyes the clock on the wall behind Maggie. "I had some things I needed to do." He glances toward Earla and Nancy, a few chairs over. "Let's get together after school. I'll meet you in the parking lot."

They're quieter than usual as they walk the path along the river. At a certain point, David says, "Come on," as he ducks off the trail, through the trees a ways, to a small clearing they've been to before.

"A little more private here," he says, as he puts his arms around her.

What she's been wanting: something to diminish the lonely distance she's been feeling since Saturday. Something to signal that they're okay. But she's wary, too; she doesn't let his hands stray today.

"What's the matter, why not?" he murmurs as he starts kissing her neck. "You were into it the other day." He's pressing up against her, pulling her in.

She says, "I don't want…"

"Why not?"

"What if I get pregnant?"

"It's okay; I'm prepared this time. You won't get pregnant."

But he senses her reluctance. "What's the matter?"

She says nothing.

"Am I supposed to read your mind or something?"

"I don't know, I just…"

"Just what?"

"I'm not ready for this."

"How can you not be ready? What's 'ready' mean? Ready how? It's the next step in where we're going, isn't it? It's hard to make out like we do and then just stop. I mean, how am I supposed to keep turning it off?"

She's looking down, her face half covered by her hair.

"I don't get it—it seems like you're into it. Why do you want to stop? Are you saying you want to break it off?"

"No! I don't want to break up, it's just…I don't know."

"Don't go all mushy on me, Maggie. It's no big deal, right? We're just hanging out together, having a good time." He laughs. "You don't look much like that little Pentecostal nerd you once were." He laughs again. "It's just the next step in the progression. You turn me on, I turn you on. Let's dig it."

She has no words to offer him. What would be the use? Nothing she would say would be what he wanted to hear.

The ground is too damp to lie down. Maggie's never seen a condom before. She's aware of him fiddling with the wrapper but is too embarrassed to watch what he's doing. She leans back against an old spruce tree until he's ready to resume, but by then all she feels is the rough bark against her back, which she can't reconcile with the sense that she has disappeared.

≈

David is moving out west with his parents. His mother has a biology degree and has decided to do graduate work in Vancouver, and since his father is a doctor, it will be easy for him to relocate as well. David is keen to go to BC. They leave at the end of June.

Maggie is lost. She has no friends. She has spent most of her free time with David for the past nine months. At least the school year has ended when he leaves; she doesn't have to face solitary days at high school.

Soon after he's gone, she dreams she is supposed to arrive at David's house in time to go with them. But she can't seem to get her suitcase packed. She is endlessly putting things into the bag, but it never gets filled. There's something she needs but she can't find it, and time goes on and on and on, and then it's too late, she's running down a street but the bag is too heavy, it slows her down. She never gets there.

≈

Late one Saturday afternoon in August, Maggie is returning home from work at the Sportsman's Grill just as her mother is arriving from a church function. When Maggie steps into the kitchen from the side door, she sees her mother standing perfectly still, her jacket half off, her head cocked to one side, facing the bedrooms. Maggie stops, wondering what has got her mother's attention, and then she hears it. A rhythmic thumping and two voices, male and female, rising together in short yelps. Her mother turns toward Maggie—"Out!" she barks, rushing at her; she seems to have twenty hands, all grabbing and pushing her. Maggie is stunned; she stumbles backward, almost falling down the three steps to the back door.

Her mother locks the door behind her. The realization of what she heard dawns on Maggie. She bangs on the door, then stops, not knowing where she wants to be, wanting/not wanting to be back inside. She can hear the harsh notes of her mother's anger, her father's drunken drawl, and a third voice, gravel laughter mixed with protest. And another sound: her own thundering heart. She steps away from the door. A blue jay screams from the maple tree, an arrow of sound aimed nowhere.

She walks to the edge of the back yard, where the forest begins— the bush that goes on forever. She's feeling sick, standing there staring into the trees. This monstrous thing he's done, it's all wrong, everything in her life is wrong. *My fucking family is a circus*, she's muttering, *a fucking ridiculous, fucking circus act. He's a clown is what he is—a stupid, fucking clown.* She aims to tell him that—*you're a fucking asshole.* Her throat aches to say it. She can taste the metallic edge of them, the words she wants to use to flay him open. Small branches that have broken off from the trees lie scattered on the ground. She picks one up and hurls it toward the bush, but there's no heft to it and it falls limply to the ground just in front of her. That's when she starts to cry. She stomps along the margin of the yard picking up bits of forest detritus—sticks and cones and bits of bark—and tries flinging them into the bush. Each time, the action fails to express her rage and she cries harder. What she needs is a brick to hurl through a window, the sound of shattering glass, the weight of the brick hitting the floor. What she needs is a mortar to fire into the house, walls crumbling, the roof collapsing, her parents unidentifiable in the rubble. She hears a ruckus near the house, voices, the door slamming. A woman staggers down the steps, struggling with the sleeves of a jacket and then giving up, bunching it into a ball and stuffing it under one arm. She sways on her feet a moment and yells at the house, "Fuckin' bitch!" and then mutters her way down the driveway.

Maggie walks into the bush, pushing through the thickest parts, branches whipping her wet face. She reaches a trail and follows it to the old mine road, then walks along it in the opposite direction from town. Gravel crunches beneath her shoes, the wind empties itself into the conifers. A raven lights in a skeletal tree, watches her. She knows this road peters out into a trail that becomes boggy and wet. She follows it as far as she can, then stops. Surveys the spindly trees, the spongy ground. This is not the way out. There's a road on the other side of town that leads to the Trans-Canada Highway, where one can turn left or right, east or west. There's a bus that can take her in either direction. All she has to do is choose.

She doesn't want to return to the house but there's nowhere else she can stay. She doesn't want to encounter either of them. She can't bear to see the set of her mother's jaw, her business-like hands. Her father's eyes turning away. When she gets home, the car is gone. In the kitchen, illuminated only by the day's waning light, her mother sits with her hands in her lap, her back to Maggie. She turns her head just enough to see from the corner of her eye that it's her daughter who's come in, then continues staring at the wall. Maggie hasn't counted on this, her mother so still and quiet. She pauses, looks at her slumped shoulders.

Eventually her mother speaks. "We all have crosses to bear; it's God's way of testing us. As Simon helped carry Christ's cross to Golgotha, we're all called to bear crosses on the road to salvation."

In the beginning was the Word. Out of nothingness, something being born. Out of darkness, light.

But the words her mother speaks: Maggie watches each one disappear into darkness.

Her mother sees her packing. "What are you doing?" Follows her to the door. "Where are you going?"

Maggie swings around in the doorway, catches a new expression in her mother's eyes. Turns her gaze back through the screen door, toward the horizon of fir spires needling the sky. "Away."

"Away where? How?"

Finding Grace

"Anywhere. I'm catching a bus."

"A bus where?" Her mother's voice more quavery than angry. Maggie isn't prepared for this. She won't turn around again. She hoists the strap of her pack higher onto her shoulder, pushes the thin latch of the aluminum screen door, hears the hinge wheeze behind her.

"Maggie," her mother tries, but the word doesn't make it through the door before it closes.

Where is she going? She's not sure. She's following a thread she's got hold of: from the fabric of her life unravelling, or a tapestry she's weaving? Nobody knows. But she's obstinate; she's got hold of that thread and she's not letting go. She's going to see where it takes her.

Iris

I SUPPOSE YOU WANT TO KNOW ABOUT THAT—what I did then, what I felt. I stepped up to the door, looked through the filmy window, rested my hand on the latch. Watched my daughter disappear down the street, every few steps shifting the load on her shoulder.

"She'll be back," I thought.

That was on a Sunday. August 16, 1974. And the next night I watched the police officer climb out of his cruiser and stare a moment at the house.

"Is this about my daughter?" I asked him at the door.

His baffled frown told me it wasn't. So I thought he had come for Hal because of some law he broke. I was ready to tell that cop I didn't know where he was, only that he was gone for good. Just to prove it, I'd show him the note I'd found that morning.

Instead, the officer had come to tell me where Hal was.

At the morgue.

The police had found him—found the two of them—on the highway where the car had slammed into a rock cut. They were headed east with a 26 of whiskey and paws they couldn't keep off each other. Maybe they were making ga-ga eyes when he lost control of the car. Or maybe she had his fly down and was working on him. Maybe he came so hard he went straight to heaven and the car just rode with him into oblivion. Maybe they both died happy.

The good news was he didn't get away without dying, so I got the insurance payoff. Maybe God was listening to my prayers all those years after all.

Not what you expected, was it. You were looking for grief—tears and snot, some open-mouthed keening, a wrecked kleenex clenched in a fist.

I can't give you that.

Instead: silence. Not mine, this time, but the silence of the world emptied out, all electric motors unplugged, combustion engines stilled. Even the birds stalled on their perches, their wings folded flat against their sides, not a feather rustling in a breeze: there is no breeze; that breathing also silenced.

Everything waiting. Like you are.

To see what I would do.

I had to identify him. Had to decide about his remains. His mortal remains, that's what they call them. The wreckage.

What happens to the unclaimed?

Do what you want with him, I said.

With great tact, they thanked me for donating his body to medical research.

What has happened to the rapture, you may ask. The song of salvation. You're wondering how I sounded in those days, what it was Dolly Baxter and my other church friends heard in my voice, what they saw in my face. Everyone looking at me carefully, trying to be surreptitious, but I'd catch them stealing glances.

No platitudes, at least. They seemed to know I didn't want any. The sheen had come off my rapture long before; people knew about my unrepentant husband, my rebellious daughter. They took my gruffness in stride, they gathered round me. Tending to a member of their flock gone lame.

In her room, all the things she didn't take. I left them there for months. The frayed teddy bear with one eye missing. In the drawers and the closet, clothes she hadn't worn for years. Old dresses I'd sewn for her, ugly things. The white baptism dress, the one she never wore again after that day with Sally Duncan. She stowed the things she rejected at one end of her closet. They hung there like accusations.

Funny how everything can stop. Everything except the clock's ticking. It's like you've reached the end of the line, the trains have stopped running and everyone else has gone home: the ticket agent, the conductor, the engineer, the baggage handlers, all the other passengers. The trains no longer wheeze and rattle. There's just you standing there on the platform, neither arriving nor leaving. There's only your pale breath in the hard November air. Snow the colour of ash in the ditch beyond the track, sky the same colour. Your hands heavy by your sides. You turn your palms up, stare at them. At the nothing they hold.

Maggie

THE BUS DOOR HISSES OPEN. SHE STEPS OFF the stale-air Greyhound into diesel fumes, the rattling drone of engines, the clang and bang of luggage compartments being opened, bags and suitcases scraping the asphalt. Her teeth chattering. Nausea and hunger: if she could manage to eat at all, she would never be able to fill the hole in her gut, it's that deep. Inside the terminal swimming in yellow light, rows of blue plastic chairs, a bank of payphones. The black receiver sweaty in her hand, a woman's voice giving directions to the YWCA.

Whenever Maggie thinks about this time, she wonders how she managed to make her way to the women's residence. How she even managed to get on the bus in Barret River and stay on it all the way to Toronto.

"Bev's tough, no doubt about it—she knifed a guy at the Four Winds last month—but if you don't give her any shit, you'll be fine," says Wanda, as she pulls back her long blond hair with its two inches of brown roots and ties it into a ponytail. Chipped red polish on her nails. "Really she's cool; she just doesn't put up with assholes." They have just emerged from the kitchen where the broad-shouldered cook glared at Maggie above the cleaver she was using to hack up a pale chicken. It's Maggie's first day on the job and Wanda's showing her the ropes.

A few days later, Wanda tells Maggie she can crash on the couch in the apartment she shares with her roommate Jill. "It'll save us rent, till you find a place." The apartment is on the second floor of an older house. Maggie sleeps on the couch in the small living room, her clothes in a box in the corner. Jill and Wanda used to work together until Jill started slinging beer at the Sidekick Lounge. "Better tips," says Jill, "especially if you flirt with the guys a bit, stand real close, lean in when you're making change. Not that I would sleep with any of those losers. But money is money." She blows a stream of cigarette smoke at Maggie. "I'm thinking of moving up to a higher-class joint— guys in suits. Not sure I want to act all hoity-toity though, so for now I'll stick with the boys in the shit-kicking boots."

Soon after she moves in, Maggie writes to David in BC.

> *Hi,*
>
> *Things here are interesting. I have a new address—in Toronto. I got the hell out of Barret. Took a bus out of there, ended up here. Feeling pretty free. I'm working at a crappy restaurant, but it's money. Staying with a couple girls, crashing on their couch for now, hanging out with them. It was good coming down by bus, the long trip, like a slow transition from my old life to my new one. It wasn't exactly like a Kerouac road trip, but it sort of had the same effect. I feel like I just woke up from a long sleep, finally living my own life. Fuck! Why did it take me so long?*
>
> *So what's happening out there in Vancouver? I bet it's pretty cool out there—and I don't mean the weather, ha ha. Maybe when I get tired of the scene here I'll take another bus trip and end up out there. Who knows? Now that I'm free, anything is possible, right?*

She signs it Maggie May, thinks David will get a kick out of that.

She's hoping he'll write back and ask why she went east instead of west.

He doesn't write back.

Maggie joins Wanda's crowd at their hangout, the Bent Nickel, a smoky bar with fluorescent lights, every second tube removed for ambience. Crotch-to-crotch moves on the dance floor, occasional fist-to-jaw moves off the dance floor, and after the bar closes, the hearty nonsense laughter drawls on at their apartment or somewhere else. Maggie's there, almost indecipherable in the smoke-haze nights and the black-coffee mornings, staggering toward another night like the one before.

There's a George. They're dancing slow; he's so tall, her head only reaches his chest. But he hunches over, rests his chin against her hair. She's small in his arms. He holds her hand as they walk back to the table, pulls his seat close, puts one arm along the back of her chair. Holds up his beer, says, "Cheers." They clink bottles and each take a swig, and then he kisses her. "I'm really into you," he says into her ear, and grins. His jeans are tight, his black shirt taut across a slight paunch. He wears a large belt buckle shaped like a transport truck cab.

He's really into her.

She's so small in the world she's almost invisible. She's terra incognita, even to herself. She couldn't position herself on a map; she needs someone else to do it for her, locate her in the too-large city. Clarify for her where she is.

That she is.

She's not sure where she fits in this new life, but for now she fits in his arms. It's something.

But it's not enough. Waking up next to his slightly flabby body in the bleary morning light, the foul taste of his mouth when he searches out hers again. The nothing they have to say to each other.

It wanes. Their attention strays; they drift apart.

Time spins on. There are other Georges, variations on a theme. The living room in Wanda and Jill's apartment officially becomes Maggie's bedroom; they all like the three-way split on rent. Maggie changes jobs from restaurant to bar waitress. The tips aren't bad. Now and then she thinks about writing home, but then she pictures the house, her mother in the kitchen, her father where? The hard silence. She's moved on; why look back?

The buses are always crowded, the streets are never still, and the city sprawls, but the size of Toronto isn't a problem after all. She has her corner of it. Her neighbourhood, the apartment she shares, the people she hangs out with. The bar where she works. It's a big city but it feels small enough, the life she's made in it.

She works, sleeps, parties. When spring arrives she walks, the sidewalks gritty with sand. There's something about the dusty light in spring, the sun climbing higher in the sky, its warmth in the cool air. No leaves yet, everything brown but brighter, not the leaden hues of winter. She wanders for a couple of hours, nowhere in particular, past brick warehouses that take up whole blocks, or through a small park.

In spring she's always restless, feels something stirring, like whatever it is beneath the still-cold ground that gets the grass to grow again. She can feel it, sitting on a park bench. She tries to zero in on it, the thing that's stirring, the thing that's possible. It's disconcerting, though: the largeness of possibility. A looming rather than an opening; more empty than full. She feels jittery, like there's something she should be doing, somewhere she should be going, something she should be planning, but she doesn't know what any of it is. It's as if she's looking around and around and around, spinning in place. If I had a pen and a piece of paper, she thinks, I could make a list. Of possibilities. Nail something down, make all the scattered thoughts more concrete. As it is, they don't quite line up in her mind. They spin off.

What do you really want to do, she asks herself.

What do you really want?

She studies the sunlight on the gnarled limbs of the trees. She studies the blue sky. The way the grass is trampled in a diagonal line bisecting the small park. She watches a ragged square of paper the slight breeze lifts and drops, lifts and drops, the stumbling progress it makes until it snags on a leafless shrub.

Maybe I should have brought a book, she thinks. I could sit here and read. She considers going to a library. Getting a library card. Pictures the rows and rows of books on neat shelves. Pictures herself standing there with no inkling of which book to choose. She remembers in grade nine having to read a book of her choice for a report. Figuring a murder mystery would at least hold her attention, she picked an Agatha Christie. Struggled through six pages before giving up. So many words, boring details, nothing she could relate to like she could the guy in *Catcher in the Rye*. There must be other books like that around; she just doesn't know what they are. She has two books David gave her: Kerouac's *On the Road*, a favourite of his. That book, in her mind, justifies the party life she's living now, imbues it with higher purpose. At least that's the general impression she gets when she cracks it open every so often. She keeps the Kerouac atop her dresser. The other book, a volume of Japanese poetry, sleeps inside a drawer.

She listens to the drone of the city, constant in the background. A car horn beeping three times, answered by one long blare from another horn. The shrill giggles of two schoolgirls walking through the park, leaning into each other. She slouches back against the bench, tilts her head toward the sun. It's her day off; there's nowhere she has to be. There's nothing she has to do. The day yawns around her. She can sit on this bench for hours, walk till dark. And nothing will have changed except the position of the sun in the sky, the length of the shadows on the ground.

"You're going to end up dumped in an alley somewhere if you don't watch out."

Maggie rolls her eyes at Jill. "I know, I know."

"I'm serious. Going off with that weirdo you met at the bar—

nobody knows the guy, and he seemed like a creep. Bullshitting about doing karate when he looked like a doughboy. What the hell made you go off with him?"

Maggie shrugs. "He was different."

"That's for sure. He seemed to be listening to voices from the goddam ceiling or something."

"Yeah, he was doing that as he was driving. It was too weird, so I got out at a red light."

Jill stares at her.

"No big deal—nothing happened."

"Don't be stupid, that's all. This isn't some little hole-in-the-wall town up north where everybody pisses in the same pot."

Maggie spins on, a wobbling top. A new guy shows up at their table at the Nickel; he works with one of the regulars. Long hair in a ponytail. Maggie's sitting beside him; he's talking about the Zen of things.

"You know about Zen? Cool." She reaches for her bottle of beer, but can't coordinate movement with vision and almost knocks it over. "Zen is so..." she waves her hand around in the air. "I kinda know about it, but it's sorta weird, eh. I'd like to hear how you define it."

"Ah, but the Zen that can be defined is not Zen." He smiles.

"Okay, then, how 'bout a vague sketch—*some*thing."

"It's everything: the what-is and the what-is-not. It's like a box. Put something into it, whatever you want. Or put nothing in. It doesn't matter. The box just is. Inside the box could be the most vivid, richest world imaginable. Or it could be as empty as the wind in that box, even if you're inside it."

Maggie nods. She's sure she knows what he's talking about, but she's drunk. Words make slow progress around her sluggish, heavy tongue. "Yeah," she drawls. "Right on. Have you ever read...fuck what's it called again." Her eyes scan the swirling room, his immaculate face hovers there, rippling close but far, and the words are swimming away. Now he's talking about the Zen of pool. "You *become* the cue, you *become* the ball. You focus down the length of the cue, your breath and all your concentration on that spot. Your mind, your breath, your energy: that's what lands the ball in the pocket."

He doesn't last long in this crowd, though. Someone hears him talking about the Zen of tennis. *Tennis!* The others tease him out of his seat at their table.

She wonders what she's doing, why she goes along like this, night after night the same group of people, all of them getting louder as the evening wears on. She drains her beer and looks around. Tinny radio music fizzles from a speaker in the ceiling, through the flat background din of human voices. Now and then a deep guffaw, a shrill giggle. Someone slurs out a Cheech and Chong routine. The table is littered with beer bottles, stubby necks above cylindrical torsos. Atop each neck a mouth, a dark o aimed blankly at the ceiling, into which someone occasionally drops cigarette ash, a spent butt.

What is, is. What is not, also is. Sometimes more loudly. A wind howling across the prairie, not even a seed in its teeth. Voluminous and empty.

She thinks about moving on.

Now and then, she thinks about that.

But then she meets Doug. Curly blonde hair making him appear more handsome than he is, his unruly teeth compensated for by the energy in his eyes, which drill through to something soft inside her and then stop drilling and waltz her instead. He's fully conversant in the language of a woman's body, his lingual talents persuasive, they drink and fuck, play games that grow more edgy with time and the more she's satiated, the hungrier she feels afterward. At the core of her is a bottomless sand pit; the unstable walls of it keep collapsing but the pit itself is never filled. Doug plans an extended business trip out west; he flies her out to meet him. It sounds romantic, a Rocky Mountain holiday, a honeymoon without the complication of marriage except for the complication of his marriage to a wife in Windsor. But he's different, somehow, this far from home; unharnessed, unfettered. Unsheathed. They drive for days through scenery they barely notice, tumbleweeds near Kamloops, the brown desert hills revealing nothing. One liquor store, one motel to another, their clothes on the floor like emptied junk-food wrappers. They don't stay in any motel longer than a single night in unspoken anticipation of complaints about the noise; one night it's their drunken crying, his wailing that he loves her after he's bitten the insides of her thighs blue.

The next night is as dark as the tar beneath them, black asphalt slick with rain. Somewhere far below, the Fraser River. Hell's Gate, he tells her. He's too drunk to drive so she's at the wheel, they're climbing a mountain pass, the road snakes up and up, she's remembering a boy who moved to BC, a boy who talked about ideas, poetry, a boy who took part of her with him. She's accelerating, the foot on the gas hers/not hers, he's telling her to slow down, red taillights slither ahead of them on the road, she pulls out to pass, he's yelling and they're accelerating, small headlights beyond suddenly as large as their windshield, she's not sure how she misses it, barely hears the truck's horn blare above his fearful shouts beside her, which only increase her speed, they're in freefall now, screaming down the other side of the mountain, passing on curves, a wall of rock on one side and on the other, nothing, nothing, nothing.

He's still shouting at her when she pulls into a motel at the end of that stretch of highway. "What's the matter with you? Are you insane? You want to get us killed—is that what you want? Go ahead then— stand on the side of the road, wait for a transport to come by, and step out in front of it. *Alone.* Leave me out of your suicide mission."

She's still holding onto the wheel, every nerve in her body vibrating. She doesn't know why she almost killed them both. She's staring at the fingers still gripping the wheel, wondering how it could be true that those are her hands. All along it's been her hands on the wheel.

Finding Grace

≈

It's not a straight line out. It's a river she navigates in the dark. One eye on the heavens, another on the silver ribbon of river lit by the moon. Though often there is no moon, there are no stars.

Grace

At age twelve, Grace desperately wanted an ant farm.

"But Mother, imagine being able to watch them inside their colony! The queen laying eggs, the workers carrying the larvae around and feeding them. I could find another ant, from outside that colony, and put it in, and we could watch how long it takes for the others to realize it's a foreign ant and start to attack it."

Her mother's mouth was open to deny the request. Then she closed it, frowned. Asked how they knew it was a foreign ant.

"Because it doesn't smell right. It doesn't have the smell of this one colony on it. Soon as the other ants realize that—whammo! They attack it."

Her mother almost looked impressed.

"And we could see when the breeding males and females are born! They have wings, and they're only born at a certain time. They fly out when it's time to mate, and they mate in the air, and then the female goes to find a place to make a new colony, and when she finds it, she breaks off her wings and starts laying eggs."

"Why does she break her wings off?"

"She doesn't need them any more. The wings are just for mating. Then she keeps a storage of the male's sperm and uses that to fertilize all the eggs she lays."

"Where did you learn all this?" A tinge of alarm in her voice.

"Mr. Humphries' *National Geographic*s that he lends me. He knows where I could order an ant farm; he gave me this catalogue."

"Let Mr. Humphries order it himself then. I'm not having ants in this house."

It was no surprise to her mother that in high school, biology was Grace's favourite class. Her teacher, Mr. Blanchet, was a lackluster man; only his dark suits were shiny from wear. Periodically he'd take his keys from his pocket and absently insert one into his ear, turn it, remove it, and clean the wax off with his fingers. Grace frequently threw him off with her questions, which arose from legitimate curiosity and were appreciated by her classmates in ways she didn't intend.

"Where do you *get* these things?" she asked, referring to the slippery pyramid of limp bullfrogs piled on a metal tray. The dissections unit of the course was under way.

Mr. Blanchet was startled.

"Is there a company that goes around killing bullfrogs and worms and things, and then sells them just so we can do this?"

"Ah, well, yes—No. They raise them; it's a biological supply company."

"They raise them? Like a worm and cricket farm, they raise them and kill them and then ship them out?"

"Well, ah. Not a farm exactly. But yes, they…process them. Preserve them in formaldehyde…."

Grace fixed her eyes on him, waiting for more.

"They have, uh, a catalogue, and I order the specimens I want."

"A catalogue! Like the Sears catalogue but full of dead things." She chortled. "Do they show pictures of the specimens—was there a picture of one of these dead bullfrogs?" She laughed again, imagining the photo of a flabby bullfrog and the short description next to it:

Bullfrog: Genuine swamp variety, black and slimy. Top quality viscera. All organs intact and clearly visible upon dissection. And maybe, *Bullfrog for Beginnners, with helpful addition of red dotted lines on underside indicating where scalpel should cut for a successful dissection.*

When Grace learned in biology that we're eighty percent water, she pictured our bodies as heavy-duty balloons filled with water, heard it sloshing up one leg and down the other as she walked. Maybe that's why whenever she put a conch shell to her ear, she heard the sea: the shell was just reflecting back what it heard inside her. Well, it wasn't surprising, since the earth was mostly oceans, and that was where life originated. Just like how we swam around in our mother's bellies like little guppies or pollywogs before we were born.

When Grace was younger, the Humphries had put pollywogs into an aquarium so she could see how they transformed from squirmy commas into frogs or toads. First the back legs appeared, then the front legs. The round body elongated and changed shape, and eventually the tail disappeared. Imagine all that going on while you're just swimming around. BOING! Out pops a leg you didn't even know you had. What did the pollywog feel just before that leg popped out? Did it get a big bulgy pain in its side? And then, whew, what a relief to know it was just a leg and not a tumor or something. But wow: a leg! Two legs! Then four legs! That must give it an entirely different sense of itself as a creature.

All the adjustments that frog would have to make, figuring out how to breathe, for one thing, and how to feed itself. What to do when winter set in. And in the spring, how the males would find their voices and females recognize their species' call, when it was time for the next batch of pollywogs to be born. All that without any parents or experienced frogs teaching them how to get along.

Maggie

MAGGIE CALLS IT THE RETREAD CENTRE but Carla objects to that name. "We're not retreads. We just got off track, but now we're back on the train." The two have been roommates since meeting at the Adult Education Centre where they're earning credits toward high school diplomas. Carla is almost thirty, several years older than Maggie, and serious about getting her diploma. A couple years before, she escaped a bad marriage, though not with every bone intact. Now she is determined to get into nursing. Maggie isn't sure what to take at college but is leaning toward office administration. She wants out of waitressing, fantasizes about a nice nine-to-five job. Working in a bright, clean office with crisply dressed, shiny-faced people, instead of coming home after work reeking of cigarette smoke and feeling vaguely sticky with french-fry grease.

She doesn't mean to, but she thinks about them. Especially since starting back to school, making this change. It's been over six years since she left. Every time an image of her mother comes into her mind, she shivers a bit. She has a harder time picturing her father. Carla is the only person she's talked to in detail about her parents, about leaving Barret River. After Maggie has mused several times about writing a letter, Carla slaps down a pen and a piece of loose leaf paper and says, "Just write the damn thing."

She puts down the date. What next? Dear Mother and Father?

Hi,

> *I know it's been a long time. I've been living in Toronto,*

*doing okay. I've been working all along, as a waitress, and
now I'm going to school part time, too.*

"How are you?" she tries aloud. Does she want to know?

I'm sorry I haven't written before. I hope you're okay.

That's enough. What else is there to say?

It sounds pathetic. Three lines on an otherwise empty page. Carla
says never mind, just mail the damn thing.

Maggie doesn't mail it. She thinks about her mother reading
it with a scowl, crumpling it into a ball and dropping it into the
garbage, her father never knowing that she wrote. She is suddenly
back in that house again, feels the chill of it, the heavy quiet, as if
there is something just about to crush it, a wrecking ball ready to
smash the house to pieces, suspended above the roof, just waiting
to drop.

It's already dropped. Years ago she walked away. She won't be
dragged back into the ruins now.

Carla and Maggie remain roommates at college, moving into a house
shared with two other women. Erin, from a small town north of the
city, studies Early Childhood Education. She's as bland and fragile as
a wafer, phones her mother each night, sniffles incessantly. Dixie, on
the other hand, is short and stocky, her hair dyed a deep, metallic red.
When Maggie first meets her, Dixie is wearing a faded black t-shirt, a
thin mauve and green silk scarf tied loosely around her neck, and lime
green tights beneath a short black skirt. She didn't get into art college
this year; she has to work on her portfolio. Meanwhile, she's studying
General Arts and Science.

Maggie thinks Dixie's pencil drawings of her family cat are good,
but she doesn't know what to make of her paintings, most of which
feature cats. She almost doesn't recognize Stonehenge, thrown off by
the garish purple and green monoliths and by the electric orange fe-
lines perched like guardians atop each lintel stone. Dixie has several

paintings of women with cat heads; one of them shows a naked cat-woman lying down with two kittens suckling at her breasts.

"Whoa, this one's weird," blurts out Maggie.

"It's a depiction of Bastet, an ancient Egyptian goddess. You haven't heard of her, obviously."

Maggie shakes her head.

"The divine mother and protectress, also known as Lady of Flame. She's considered both a good mother and a ferocious defender of the sun-god Ra, so she has two sides to her personality—both docility and aggression."

"Oh."

"Some even relate her in some way to the famous goddess Isis."

"Isis?"

"The universal mother—the mother and protector of the Pharaoh, goddess of magic and nature."

Maggie tries to look impressed.

"The Egyptians knew a thing or two about cats; there's more to them than most people think."

Erin always wears a panicked smile in Dixie's presence; Carla just rolls her eyes and tells Dixie to get real. Maggie tolerates her, though, and mostly finds her amusing. She's only six years older than Dixie, but in the younger woman's presence she feels leathery-old, and plain as a pair of brown oxfords. She sits through Dixie's mini-lectures about art—what it is, what it isn't, what it's supposed to be—and eventually Dixie offers to give her a quick art history tour at the art gallery.

Maggie's never been to a gallery before, and she's intimidated by the size of this one, the high-ceilinged lobby where everyone but her seems to know the routine of buying tickets, checking bags, and then finding their way to whatever is inside. She's relieved to have Dixie as her guide, even though she cringes at the volume with which Dixie pontificates. Maggie nods and says "Hmm" a lot, until they reach a collection of paintings that are unexpectedly familiar. Bleak straggly trees and a chaos of light and colour; bald rocks beneath an ocean of sky. Something shifts in her stomach. Somewhere outside her, a bass string has been plucked, and the drum of her diaphragm cradles the note, vibrates with it. It's not visual or aural; it's visceral.

But Dixie is impatient to move on, dismissing this collection as cliché Canadiana. Maggie trails Dixie out of the room with her head turned back, looking over her shoulder, trying to sort out what just happened in there.

Maggie muses about photography. They have a program at the college, she tells Carla. It sounds more interesting than office work. She likes taking pictures.

"How are you going to pay the bills with photography?" asks Carla. "You want to spend your life being bossed around by snippy-faced brides in big white dresses—or worse, their mothers?"

"You're just biased against weddings on account of your own marriage."

"You got that right."

"But weddings aren't the only option. I could do nature photography or something."

"Nobody'll pay you to take pictures of trees."

"Unless I take really good ones."

"Maggie, you talk about how you wasted the last six or seven years of your life. So now you plan to waste another five or ten? You say you want out of waitressing, but you'd have to keep on waiting tables to support your photography career." Carla traces quotation marks in the air around the last word. "What's wrong with office admin? A job in an office would be better than waitressing."

"That's what I thought. But I don't know, it's kind of boring."

"Try nursing then; it's not boring, it's just overwhelming."

Maggie grimaces. "I could never be a nurse."

"Why not?"

"I don't know. I'd never be sure I was doing the right thing, I'd worry I'd kill somebody. At least in an office when I make mistakes it won't be life-threatening."

Carla shrugs. "You do your best, that's all."

"But honestly, how would you deal with somebody dying when you're supposed to be caring for them?"

"People die. And just because they die it's not necessarily your fault. People get sick, or they have accidents, and they die. Doctors and nurses aren't miracle workers. There's always somebody going to die."

"I guess so. But no nursing for me. All that science you take."

"It's not bad. But you're more airy-fairy than a science type."

"Airy fairy?"

"Your head in the clouds. Always wondering about things, why things are the way they are. Science would be too practical for you."

"What do you mean always wondering about things?"

"Like just last week when you and Dixie were talking about fate and chance and whether there's a path we're supposed to be following. A whole lot of hooey."

"What's wrong with thinking about that kind of thing?" Maggie exclaims.

"Won't pay the rent, won't get you a diploma. And it won't change a damn thing in the world."

≈

Near the completion of her office administration diploma, Maggie meets Sam through Dixie. She's struck by his strong, unusual face: the prominent bridge of his nose arguing with sharp cheekbones, the jutting jaw vying for attention, and pale blue eyes that seem to calm all that commotion. Like Maggie, Sam seems to enjoy Dixie's tirades about art.

"Like in photography," Dixie is saying. "You know about this, Sam, you're a photography student. Black and white is the only way to go. Colour film should be outlawed. At least then people wouldn't be so inclined to snap sunsets. 'Oh look!'" she mimics. "'Ooohhh, it's orange! Wow, now it's red! Ooohhh, even the clouds are pink!' God. If they outlawed colour, we wouldn't have to put up with forty million pictures of sunsets that are all the same." She fixes her eyes on Sam. "You ever snap a sunset?"

He throws both hands in the air in mock self-defense. "Who me? I wouldn't be caught dead with a sunset in my portfolio." He grins. "And cats neither. No sunsets or cats."

Dixie sits bolt upright. "Don't you ever put those two in the same category. Have you ever owned a cat? Obviously not. I think for that portrait assignment of yours, you should use cats instead of humans. Now that would be interesting—capturing cat intelligence and wisdom in a series of portraits."

"Maybe in colour, with a sunset in the background," offers Maggie.

"I'd like to shoot you, if you don't mind." He laughs at her reaction. An easy laugh. "That's photographer-speak." He explains about his portrait assignment, asks if she'll be a subject.

Maggie eyes him warily.

"*Portraits*, not nudes. You get to remain fully clothed. I just set up different types of lighting, get you to stand this way and that."

"Why me?"

"I don't know. The shadows around your eyes."

She likes the way he stops and thinks. Stands still with a finger on his lip, his eyes moving slowly around the room. "How about..." he'll muse, getting her to position her head and body just so, then alternately peering through the lens and fiddling with the lights.

"Where are you from?"

"Uh, Barret—"

"Don't look right at me or the camera. Keep looking over there. How do you like school?"

Pause.

Click.

"Good—don't answer my questions as I ask; just think about the answers. What's your favourite kind of music?" *Click.*

"Where do you want to be in your life in ten years?" *Click.*

Maggie imagines what this photo will reveal: her face an absolute blank.

"Think about yourself, age six." *Click.* "Now age sixteen." He snaps the shutter several times.

Over coffee later he asks, "So what was going on in your life when you were sixteen?"

"What did your photographer's eye tell you?"

"Chaos."

"That's about right."

"Tell me again where you grew up?"

"Barret River. North of Lake Superior."

"The boonies."

"Yup."

"What was it like growing up there? Now you can answer with words instead of facial expressions."

"Not great."

"That's all? Not great?"

He's drawn to mysteries. Her watchfulness, the way she seems to be observing things from a distance, or from deep inside. She's like an image in the darkroom just as it's appearing, as if it gets arrested at that point. Faint; there but not there.

At the pub one night he talks about his family—his one sister, his mother's death from cancer a few years ago, how difficult that was, how much closer it brought him and his sister and father. Maggie listens quietly, tries to imagine such a life. When he asks about her family, she's vague, says she's an only child. She turns the conversation away from her past, gets him to tell her more about the place where he grew up. When she asks how he became interested in photography, he talks about how he likes capturing images that tell a story. An enigmatic expression on someone's face, for example. They're outside now, both affected by the beer. He stops, puts a hand on her arm. He's standing close, studying her. "Like your face, very enigmatic," he says, and then they're kissing and she hasn't been in anyone's arms for so long and not someone like him, and she's almost ready to open like the Georgia O'Keefe flowers Dixie showed her.

Almost but not quite.

He's completely comfortable in his skin. She learns he often acts as a model for figure-drawing classes, and when Dixie tells her he's a favourite model, Maggie knows why: his exquisitely proportioned and sculpted body, not anything you'd guess at when he's clothed. A fine line of hair running from his navel down, like a seam. She loves to watch him rise from the bed naked in the morning, stride across the room to the bathroom and then return again. She drinks in every inch of him. And when he stretches his body out along the length of hers, it doesn't matter what he does—where he places his warm palm, what part of her he traces with a fingertip or explores with his tongue. She has never drunk so deeply at this well. He's unabashed and tender, kisses her bewildered tears, the ones she can't explain. To make her smile, he puts his eye up against her cheek and bats his eyelashes so she feels the flutter of the lashes against her skin. "Butterfly kisses," he says, chuckling. "My mom used to do that when we were little, give us butterfly kisses."

Maggie has a big exam one day at noon. At 8:00 that morning, Sam knocks on the door. He has biked over, and unloads from his backpack a bag of flour mixture for pancakes, an apple, and a single egg stowed carefully in newspaper inside a plastic container. Even Carla's face softens as she watches him gently extract the egg from its nest.

"Wanted to be sure you had a good breakfast before your exam. Go ahead and do what you have to do. I'll just cook up some pancakes and then get out of your hair."

Two weeks later, when Maggie gets a full-time position at the college, Sam prepares a special celebratory meal, and the next day he leaves town. He has one year left in his photography program, but he's got a summer job at a provincial park near Ottawa, and is gone for three months. He's able to get back to Toronto only one weekend that summer; otherwise, they talk on the phone periodically.

When he returns in late August, they're initially a bit shy, aware of a sneaking realization that they don't really know each other that well.

"I bet you're a good card player. You play cards?"

Maggie frowns. "Not really. Why?"

"Good poker face. Nobody'd ever guess you had a royal flush up your sleeve."

She smirks, shakes her head.

"It's true." He takes her face between his hands, looks into her eyes. "What's going on in there? That's what I want to know."

"I'll never tell."

"I have ways," he chuckles and kisses each of her eyelids, "of making you talk."

"Hmmmm. Keep trying."

Her subterfuge works for awhile. But not long after he returns, things begin to fray. Sam finally draws out Maggie's story about leaving Barret River.

"You're not in touch with your parents at all? You've never gone back? Not once?"

She shakes her head.

"Why not?"

"Why go?"

He's taken aback. "To see your parents—how they're doing. To see your home town."

"Why would I want to return to all that? My life there was crap. My parents were losers; they had nothing to offer me then and that won't have changed. They were hopeless."

"What do you mean, hopeless?"

"I'm telling you, my mother was a fanatic. I mean insanely fanatic. Jesus Christ was all she cared about; she didn't care about me or my father."

"What about him?"

"He was a drunk. Screwing-around-in-the-house-with-another-woman drunk. I'd had it with both of them. I wanted out and I got out. Why go back to all that?"

"People change. Maybe they've changed."

She rolls her eyes. "You never met them. You have a real family, with normal people in it, so it's hard for you to imagine growing up alone with two losers for parents."

"I guess. But still—I think I'd be curious about them, at least. I'd just want to see."

"Why?"

"Why not?"

"*Why not* doesn't answer the question. Why would you want to see?"

"In case they had changed. Or maybe they're dead, or one of them is."

"So if they're dead, there's nothing to see."

"You wouldn't want to know?"

"Sam, what you don't get is that *I don't care.*"

He scrutinizes her, leans back in his chair. "I think I'm starting to get that."

In his eyes, what is that?

He talks a lot about his wonderful, stimulating time at the park—his second summer there working in the visitors' service program. Living in park lodgings with other staff, some returned from last year and some new. A lively and interesting and somewhat crazy bunch, he's got a million hilarious anecdotes—the tiny sauna they built out of an old outhouse, the evenings spent hooting for owls, the crazy old logger character he played in a skit they put on for the campers. And someone named Judith who worked with him: he talks about her a bit too much. Why can't her name just be *Judy*, grumbles Maggie to herself, instead of the goddess-sounding Judith?

Maggie becomes greedy, jealous of everything in his life. Even the way he talks about his father and sister, who came out from Ottawa for a couple days; the wonderful time he spent with them at someone's rustic cottage on the Rideau River. A weekend of endless conversation and scrabble games and lying on a dock with his sister beneath a starry sky, awed by an amazing meteor shower. She envies him the life he has. The unbearable sun-drenched goodness of it, the people in it, the connections he has with all of them.

Maggie has trouble imagining herself in that life. She's an ungainly foal bewildered by its legs: comical or pathetic, or both. Not to be taken seriously.

Sam's sister greets her with a lingering handshake, placing a second hand on top of Maggie's. "I'm so glad to meet you, Maggie." She speaks slowly and intently, as if everything depends on what she says and how she says it. Maggie notices a silver bangle on Elena's wrist and dangly silver and turquoise earrings.

"Good to meet you, too," says Maggie, withdrawing her hand. She looks breezily around the room. "Smells good, Sam; what are you cooking?" She's aware of Elena's eyes on her.

"Pasta primavera," announces Sam. "Glass of wine?"

The three of them go into the kitchen. "So, Maggie, I hear you work at the college." Elena wears a warm, welcoming, extremely irksome expression that says she wants to know everything about her brother's girlfriend. Maggie hates that look; it makes her want to grow fur and howl.

"And I hear you're a counsellor," Maggie replies.

Elena smiles, nods. After it's clear Maggie isn't probing further, she offers, "At a women's shelter."

"Yeah, Sam told me that." Maggie takes a sip of wine. Elena glances at her brother, smiles more weakly this time.

"How do you like working at the college?" Elena tries again.

"It's okay. Nothing special, really. I work as a clerk in the Learning Assistance Centre."

"So you're interacting with students a fair bit? That must be interesting."

"Some days more than others." Maggie's neck is hot and prickly. She can feel herself resisting, clamming up. She doesn't know why. She can't look at Sam, knowing she'll see puzzlement or dismay in his eyes. The conversation limps along, but it feels as if there's something grotesque perched on her shoulder that they're all trying their best to ignore.

Maggie doesn't hear from Sam for a few days, and she doesn't call him. When he does phone, he says he'd like to come by for a coffee.

At first he's looking everywhere but at her. Neither of them attempts small talk as she places the mugs on the kitchen table.

"Where do you see yourself in another year or two, Maggie?"

She's floored by the question. "Um…a couple years from now, wow." She pauses, then tries to divert his attention with humour. "Wait till I pull out my crystal ball and have a look," she says, pretending to rummage though a stack of papers on the table.

He's waiting.

"I don't know...how should I know? It took me awhile to get where I am now, so I guess I'm coasting a bit for the time being."

"What's important to you?"

She's a deer caught in headlights. "Whoa. You don't waste any time getting into the heavy stuff."

He is not being deterred.

"Maybe you could have prepared me in advance for this line of questioning," she tries. Then, "Um...what's important to me. Well, being honest, being a good person, working hard...."

"What about relationships?"

It's not fair, these open-ended questions. "Yeah, relationships are important..." Can she say it? *You* are important—my relationship with you is important?

After a minute, he says, "Look, Maggie, I'm not sure this is going anywhere. I mean you and me. I kind of think we're at a dead end."

Dead end?

"I think I'm looking for something different in a relationship than you are."

Different how? She keeps her eyes glued to the coffee in front of her, the thin slick of cream on the surface of it.

"I'm sorry I wasn't great with your sister," she blurts out, talking fast now, her eyes darting around the room. "I don't know what was wrong with me, I wasn't myself, I didn't mean to be so...I don't know, rude or something. We could have another chance—." She sees him watching her.

She's crazy about him. She is.

He reaches across the table, touches the back of her hand. "Maggie," he says quietly. "It's not going to work."

~

Maggie and someone, maybe Sam, were supposed to meet somewhere. A park or something, a wide green space. That's what she thought. She's in that park, but no Sam or whoever. Then a panicked thought—maybe this was not the rendezvous point they'd arranged; maybe she was supposed to stay where she'd been, where she'd come from, and he would meet her there. She starts to walk back, along a narrow dirt road or path bordered by dark trees. She's got something in her arms, a heavy bundle, a sack full of clothes or something bulky. It's hard to carry, it slows her down, but she can't let go of it—she's not allowed to leave it at the roadside, she's not sure why. Everything depends on getting to the designated meeting place, where the person is waiting. Sam?—she's not even sure if it's him she's supposed to be meeting. The road goes on and on, she keeps putting one foot ahead of the other, the ground is uneven, it feels like she's going the wrong way on an escalator, she's making no progress. It's growing darker as she walks, she's feeling more and more hopeless. Bereft. At some point the bundle is a child, that's why she couldn't just put it down, abandon it. A child one or two years old she's carrying in her arms, the child as bereft and distressed as she is, she's got her nose in the child's hair, the familiar sleepy smell of it makes her ache, and then she's awake, still feeling the heft of that child in her arms, pressed against her chest.

When she's awake and thinking about the dream, she wonders why she didn't just ditch the bundle at the roadside, unburden herself of it. That child. She could have left it behind.

≈

It's not just a guilty pleasure; it's some kind of need. And the secrecy is important: doing it without getting caught. She can manage entire pies only when she knows Carla won't be home. They're sharing an apartment again, just the two of them. When Carla is working evenings, Maggie will buy a banana cream pie, thinking she'll eat just one slice and leave the rest in the fridge, share it with Carla. All the way home from the bakery, she's thinking about this pie; she feels jittery with anticipation, can't wait to get it out of its package and put the first forkful of it into her mouth, let its comforting, despicable creaminess linger there before swallowing it, knowing there's more. Knowing she has six hours till Carla gets home. She could even go back and buy a second pie if she needed to—but not at the same shop; someone might remember she'd just been there.

Before she knows it, she's eaten half the pie, and then she panics, wondering how to explain this to Carla, too embarrassed to admit gorging herself. So she has to decide: finish the second half now, or hide it in her room, unrefrigerated. And how to dispose of the foil pie plate and the bulky plastic cover? She'll have to put it in a separate garbage bag and dump it into the bin outside. Destroy the evidence.

It's this anxious guilt she's aiming for. It's like putting herself through a shredder, having her skin ripped off in long, thin strips. Why does it feel like relief? A buildup of panic, a kind of manic intensity, followed by catharsis: there, it's done. Another whipping. It's finished now until the next time she needs to do this to herself. And there's also the physiological effect of the sugar-and-fat indulgence. That lethargy, afterward. Anesthesia.

She's angry at her parents for the life they gave her. How is she supposed to be normal, when that's what she was born into, that household? She managed to escape, but not soon enough. She's tainted. The stench of their misery permeates her. Sam could smell it; that's what drove him away. So she's renovating, starting with the foundation. The excavation is complete; now she's backfilling with something sublime: cream pies, butterscotch cheesecakes, chocolate eclairs frilled with whipped topping, the more of it the better, lulling her into sleepiness, where she can dream herself complete.

Ascetics practise mortification of the flesh as a religious discipline, to move beyond the physical realm and into a spiritual one. Maggie is doing the opposite: indulging the flesh, mortifying the soul.

Grace

THEY PULL OFF THE HIGHWAY ONTO A NARROW DIRT ROAD that winds down to a small clearing by the lake—just enough space to turn the vehicle around. A short trail through spruce and pine leads to the beach: a long, shallow crescent of smooth, bright cobbles. The sun burns the last of the morning mist from the bay, gradually revealing a massive rocky headland to the north, the granite's pink somehow muting its presence. It doesn't look real; it's as if someone has painted a soft pastel watercolour mural out in this wind-battered place.

Kaia and Eric drive out here with Grace a few times a year; Kaia calls it their pilgrimage. They walk the length of the beach, stopping every few steps to admire rocks. Too many to take home, but they fill their pockets. Pale green and deep green, chalk white and solid black, pink and red, blue and turquoise and grey, some with stripes or crosses or lightning zig-zags, some mottled every colour. The whole effect is brightness; the beach seems to glow with light thrown up by the cobbles that are smooth and rounded from being washed and tossed again and again by the waves. Driftwood, like bleached bones, lies scattered along the shore—entire trees, some with roots still attached, heaved ten metres up to the base of the dune bordering the beach. She'd love to have been here when the lake was that rough, to see the size and fury of waves that could toss whole trees as if they were playing a giant's game of pick-up-sticks.

But today Lake Superior is sleeping, deep blue in the May sunlight.

116

Finding Grace

At the end of the beach they pick up a trail that follows the shore-line, meandering into the bush and then out onto the rocky shore, back and forth between sunlight and shade, bare rock and needle-strewn earth. When they reach the tip of the headland, by tacit agree-ment, they each wander to a separate spot and sit awhile looking out over the wide, wide water. Here, the rock sprawls down to the water's edge like a spent elephant: great grey humps and lumps, with a leg or two sloping into the clear water. But it's not just plain elephant-grey. In some places the granite is swirled through with charcoal stripes; in others it's been stained deep ochre or washed a pale pink, or splashed with bright lichens: electric orange, lime green. Long tongues of sat-iny black basalt flow like rivers through the granite, as if it's still in liquid form, as if the earth hasn't cooled yet.

Such a long history is stored in these rocks—imagine everything they've seen over four billion years! First is the drama of birth. It's especially clear along the north shore of this lake, where the land hunches up in great jagged humps and ridges, forested but often showing what it's made of in exposed, dark cliff faces where even acrobat cedars can't hang on. Igneous bedrock: born of fire in the earth's belly and heaved up into ornery hills and ridges and outcrops. Just looking at it you know it had a traumatic birth: it's all fractured geometry, tortured trigonometry, uneven angles piled and wedged into each other, nothing smooth or calm or sine-wave about it except right along the shore where the water has soothed its ragged edges.

That's bedrock geology: the forces that shaped the backbone billions of years ago. But since then, the rocks have undergone topo-graphic surgery, thanks to glaciers dragging themselves back and forth across the land. The last glacier was at its peak 20,000 years ago, and it wasn't until 7,000 years ago that it had receded to reveal the new shape of things. An extended facelift, chuckles Grace; hope that cos-metic surgeon wasn't charging by the hour!

The best part of the rock is near the water's edge, where it's been worn skin-smooth by wave after wave after wave. Grace kneels and runs her hands over it, lays her face against the rippled rock to feel the smoothness of it on her cheek. It's remarkable that something as insubstantial as water can have this effect. How much time had to go by for the waves to do this? Too much to even imagine. Relative to that span of years, the hours she'll spend here today will be smaller than the nucleus of an atom in the cell of the tissue making up the toenail on a gnat. If gnats had toenails. And she's that small, too. Somehow it makes her happy, to feel so miniscule, almost invisible. Microscopic. Microscopic doesn't mean insignificant: just think of the flu virus or salmonella bacteria. Think of the plankton in the sea—the basis of all life in the whole, entire ocean. And the oceans being the thing that makes Earth unique in the solar system.

That's pretty significant.

After a while, the three of them converge again and unpack the lunch they've brought. Kaia watches the swells fill a small hollow in the rock and then drain out again. She points it out to Grace and Eric. "Filling and emptying. That's what I always feel here, what this place does. Fills me and empties me."

Kaia, sitting cross-legged, made of stone—not exactly her, but a form vaguely human, a hint of outstretched arms, a rounded back, so the torso is cave-like, the hollow of her lap polished smooth. Grace can see the sculpture in her mind but she doubts she could make it. But if she could, she'd place it at the water's edge somewhere along this shore, where the waves could wash through it. There are already sculptures like that all along here, where water has carved out hollows and polished edges smooth. But it's the vague resemblance to a human that's compelling, a human form with lake water sieving through it. A human form subject to erosion by water: something we can't even hold in our hands for long.

"I wonder... If the waves can smooth out rock like this, I wonder how long it would take, if you sat on that rock there, just at the water's edge—I mean, if it was possible for someone to just sit there that long without dying of starvation—I wonder how long it would take for the water to erode your skin right off?"

Eric groans. "Count me out of *that* experiment."

It's true: flesh is a pretty messy medium.

Maggie

SHE DREAMS SHE HAS GORGEOUS IRIDESCENT blue-green feathers growing out from the corners of her mouth, and she touches them in wonder at their beauty, amazed that something so remarkable should be part of her. And suddenly she sees them in a different light, as something freakish and ugly: people are not supposed to grow feathers. So she snips them off with scissors, but the stiff butts of the quills are still visible at the corners of her lips. Now she feels more grotesque than before because nothing remains of the feathers' original beauty and colour; now she has only these large stiff bristles at the corners of her lips.

Grace

A BABY GRACKLE HAS FALLEN OUT OF ITS NEST and is squatting on the lawn. Its parents hop over to it, squawk in its face, then turn and fly. They do this over and over and over again, trying to teach it to get airborne. People have a tendency to say that animals engaged in parenting behaviour are like humans. But it's really the other way around: people are more like animals, like those grackles doing their best, often not very sophisticated at all. Awkward and rudimentary. Hopefully the offspring are able to obtain nourishment and avoid predators. Often that's as far as it goes; that's the extent of what their parents can teach them. How to eat and avoid getting eaten.

You can't deny that we're animals; just one species of mammal. But it's true we're different from other animals, too. Take reproduction, for instance. Humans are so obsessed with love and romance—all those magazine articles about how to woo a mate, and the countless stories of movie stars hopping from bed to bed. Every week there's a new jilted and famously weeping lover. Other animals don't get so bent out of shape about sex; they just get down to business. Listen to the frogs in spring: they know what mating is all about. The spring peepers, especially; they go into a frenzy in May. There must be a million of them in the marsh, chirping so loud it hurts Grace's eardrums. A full chorus of sex-starved peepers can reach 120 decibels—that's as loud as a chain saw! And in terms of biological reproduction, shadflies take the cake. Except they couldn't *eat* the cake, because they have no mouths. All shadflies do, once they get to the adult stage, is mate and

121

then die: no question there about the imperative for reproduction, for the life of the species to go on, even though you could question the worth of a life such as that.

It could be argued that humans have bigger lives than shadflies; at least we have mouths and stomachs, which is a start. Humans also have ambitions and dreams, which shadflies seem to lack—just look at them sit on a window doing nothing for two days until they die. And what about making things that serve no practical purpose: what about art? Kaia's sculptures, Eric's paintings, Grace's own creations. What are they about? They have nothing to do with digestive or re-productive systems. They're not about attracting a mate or keeping the lions at bay. They're more about seeing, and communicating what you see in a language that doesn't get all hung up on words and tone.

Or sometimes it's about what you don't see. Like the installation she calls Maggie's Door. It's more something felt. Like there's an-other being inside you that has something to say you hadn't thought of yourself, something kind of big to say. Your hands do its bidding. With the door, all Grace did was think about Maggie. The questions that couldn't be answered—couldn't even be asked. Things like that well up in you and next thing you know you're making something that will empty you out. And then the object itself becomes something more than questions or answers. Maggie's Door is like a shrine; it's comforting to have something concrete, something kind of alive, even if what it mostly represents is absence.

Maggie

STANDING IN FRONT OF A LARGE, CLUTTERED METAL DESK is a trim man of medium height, with short black hair. Heavy shadow where he's shaved. His dark brown eyes attempt seriousness but can't quite help dancing.

"Good day, good day; I am Fareed." Given his stature, the voice is surprisingly loud; it seems to bound around the room. He motions to a middle-aged woman sitting in a chair beside the desk. She doesn't make a move to shake Maggie's hand, but nods repeatedly while smiling at her.

"This is my wife, Jamila."

"Hello, glad to meet you," says the woman, her voice deep and rich like coffee.

A cardboard carton with papers sticking up out of it sits on the only other chair in the room. Fareed glances around, lifts the box and deposits it atop a filing cabinet. "Please, sit," he says, indicating the chair, which is set against the wall, at right angles to the desk and Jamila. As Maggie moves hesitantly toward the chair, Jamila says, "Fareed, the chair," waving her hand in Maggie's direction.

"Yes, yes," he says, pulling the chair out from the wall and turning it to face them. He holds an open palm toward the chair, saying to Maggie, "Thank you very much. Thank you."

Maggie sits down while Fareed searches for a place to sit himself and ends up perched on the edge of the desk. "So," says Fareed. "Thank you for coming to Haddad Enterprises."

Maggie blinks. "You're welcome. Thank you."

They both smile at her.

Layoffs at the college where Maggie has been working have forced her to look for a new job, and her first two interviews have been unsuccessful. But this interview is not at all like the others. It seems to Maggie that it takes Fareed and Jamila a long time to get down to business. They appear content to engage in a lot of small talk.

How long have you lived in Toronto?" asks Fareed.

"About fifteen years."

"This is a nice city," says Jamila.

"Yes, better than Beirut!" exclaims Fareed. "At least here, the buildings are still standing."

"Bayroot?"

"That is where we are from," explains Jamila.

"Oh," Maggie nods, trying to remember where that is.

"But now we are here, thank God, and not in the middle of civil war!" cries Fareed.

Maggie is beginning to realize that they want her to participate in this pre-business chit-chat. "How long have you been here?"

"Eighteen years," Jamila replies.

"Oh," says Maggie. "That's a long time."

"Some days it feels a long time; other days I think we just arrived."

"Until we look in the mirror," exclaims Fareed. "Then we realize how old we have become, here in Canada!"

"Or we look at our three daughters, especially our youngest, Myriam. Except she is away now, at university in British Columbia." She pauses, smiling at Maggie, giving her a chance to participate.

"Uh, yes... How old is she?"

"Twenty years. Our baby."

"Our *baby*," Fareed mocks. "Twenty is not a baby! But she won't grow up." He grins at Jamila, who bats an arm at him.

"You spoiled her, that is why!" exclaims Jamila. She nudges Maggie's arm. "He spoiled her, his little girl. Always, he gives her what she wants."

Fareed throws his hands in the air, says to Maggie, "Listen to her." He looks at his wife. "Who was with her all the day? It was not just me that spoiled her."

Jamila is laughing. "We love all our girls. But the baby is always the baby. You can't change that, you know? You just can't."

It becomes clear during their conversation why the office is cluttered. They are in the process of moving the business into this new office space with its attached warehouse to accommodate the increased volume of goods that Fareed imports and then ships out to customers. He has developed a very successful business importing Middle Eastern foodstuffs that he delivers to small grocers and restaurants. Demand for those goods has grown steadily, and now he is adding textiles and home décor items from the Middle East and Asia. Jamila has been doing the bookkeeping, but because the business is expanding, he needs additional office staff.

Only one of Maggie's answers during their conversation seems to cause Fareed and Jamila concern. They exchange a quick glance, and then Fareed squints with incomprehension.

"No family," he says. "None? No sisters, no brothers? No aunts, no—"

"Fareed, she already said," interrupts Jamila, who is watching Maggie closely.

"None," shrugs Maggie. She smiles, trying to make them feel better.

"It's all right, don't worry. Eh, Fareed?" She pulls her eyes away from Maggie to look at her husband, placing a hand on his arm.

At the end of the interview, Jamila nods at Fareed, who then booms, "Yes, yes. So everything is fine. When can you begin?"

After Maggie has been working for the Haddads for a few weeks, she reluctantly accepts an invitation to dinner at their home. She enters a dimly lit living room, the curtains drawn to reduce the glare on the television, where a car chase is in progress. Fareed greets her enthusiastically and introduces her to his father, his mother, and the little grandson sitting on her lap. Fareed's parents both smile and nod at her, and then the two men exchange a few words in Arabic. His mother resumes speaking to the boy on her knee, playing some kind of rhyme or game involving his hands that she says over and over to make him giggle. When Jamila appears, wearing an apron, the grandson runs over and wraps his arms around her leg. She takes the boy by one hand and Maggie by the other, and leads them out of the living room, ignoring Fareed's loud protests about Maggie being a guest. In the hallway, they encounter Jamila's son-in-law, Rob, who's being tugged along by his four-year-old daughter, Carmella. Before she knows it, Maggie's in the kitchen being greeted by the Haddads' daughters, tall Leyla with a wild mane of long, black curls, and short Amal whose broad smile reveals brilliant white teeth. Amal hands Maggie a knife and places her in front of a huge mound of parsley. "It has to be fine; cut it up good and fine or Mama will put you out in the street! Eh Mama?"

Leyla chastizes Amal for giving the guest the worst of the kitchen chores. "Mama—the parsley! Amal gave her parsley job to Maggie! You don't have to do that if you don't want. Here—want to squeeze lemons instead?"

Jamila laughing through all of this, hoisting the two-year-old onto her hip and feeding him something—rice?—with her fingers. Carmella running back and forth between kitchen and living room, screaming with laughter, being chased around by Rob. "It's terrible we make you work," shouts Jamila above the ruckus. "But it's better here than the living room—the kitchen is where the fun is. Isn't that right, my girls?"

"I'm having a lot more fun now that Maggie's cutting the parsley!" exclaims Amal. "How 'bout you, Maggie—aren't you having a blast?"

The heat in the bright kitchen, the constant chatter of the women, the screams and giggles of the children, the adults in the other room talking loudly while tires squeal and sirens wail on the television, the tang of garlic and lemon, the sizzling meat, the mossy smell of parsley on the green-stained cutting board. Leyla carving cloves of garlic into thin slices and then WHAM, smashing the heel of her hand down on the flat side of the chef's knife, crushing the garlic beneath it. "Mmmm," she says at one point, holding her fingers up to her nose. "I'll have this smell of garlic on my fingers for another day or so, reminding me of this meal." She looks at Maggie hopefully. "Do you like garlic?"

"Um..."

"Not sure?" cries Amal, in mock shock.

"You'll know tonight whether you do or not," laughs Leyla. "You'd better be a convert!" she says, waving the knife in the air. "If not, the world will come to an abrupt end."

It becomes a standing invitation for Maggie to have supper at Jamila and Fareed's on Sundays. At first she's not sure they really want her there. And it's work, socializing with them. It would be easier to stay home alone, fry some eggs for supper, eat in front of the television. But because Fareed is her boss, she's not comfortable refusing their hospitality.

Most Sundays, the whole family is there, just like the first time. After a few weeks, Jamila and her daughters are hugging Maggie hello and goodbye. She's startled by this, feels like she's in the subway at rush hour, jostled down the line of the three women—except that they're smiling, not frowning, and their arms are extended instead of elbowed out. She has to learn how to hug back, relax her body and receive the embrace rather than stiffen against it.

She gets geography and history lessons from the Haddads. When it's clear she's not really sure where Lebanon is, Fareed pulls out the atlas. "You work for Haddad Enterprises, you must know where Lebanon is at least—and other countries we import from!" He rambles on about the Ottoman Empire and colonialism, Muslims, Druze and Maronites, the PLO and Israel. It's too much new information and she has no context for it, has trouble relating all the pieces to each other. She can't keep straight who's who.

"Don't worry!" exclaims Fareed. "Half of them over there, they don't know who they are fighting or why. Even those supposed to be on the same side fight each other. They are all just crazy!"

Maggie hears about how things were heating up in the late 60s, early 70s, when they came to join Fareed's brother in Toronto. "But things are getting better there now," says Jamila. "Settling down. Now maybe they can start to rebuild."

"Rebuild—that will not be easy." Fareed shakes his head. "Beirut was a jewel before—the Paris of the Middle East! Now destroyed. Buildings fallen down, bombed, the walls still standing are full of bullet holes. A pile of rubble." He scowls, throws his hands in the air.

≈

"Are you kidding? What have I been reading lately?" says Amal in response to Myriam's question. The youngest sister is home for a visit, and even though it's not Sunday, Maggie is at Haddads' for a special family dinner. Everyone has been eager for Maggie and Myriam to meet.

"*Horton Hears a Who* and *Thomas's Snowsuit*, that's about where I'm at," says Amal.

"Amal," chides Leyla, "you haven't introduced the kids to Tolstoy yet? What's the matter with you?"

"Or Elias Khoury," quips Myriam. "Something culturally relevant, at least."

"Snowsuits are extremely relevant in this culture," says Leyla.

Myriam laughs. "Leyla to the defence. Okay, so what about you? No kids for an excuse. And please don't tell me you're reading tort law at bedtime."

"Well, it almost puts me to sleep, so it's at least useful in that regard. But no, I do get in other reading—bits at a time, though. I'm almost finished *News from a Foreign Country Came*."

Myriam squints. "I think I've heard of that..."

"It's pretty intense. I won't say any more about it, though, or I'll give too much away. You should read it."

Myriam is reading *Happy Days* by Beckett, after having seen the play. Leyla wants to know what it's about.

"Existential blight, what else? It's Beckett. And it's amazing. Basically a one-woman play, two acts. In the first act, she's buried up to her waist in a sand heap. And in the second act, she's buried up to her neck."

Leyla looks skeptical. "Sounds riveting."

"It was mesmerizing; the actress was so strong. And the play itself, Beckett's writing, blew me away. All about how we grope for meaning in the most banal things, or how we desperately try to avoid seeing the inherent meaninglessness in our lives by busying ourselves with trivial matters. It's the best play I've seen for awhile."

Amal is grimacing. "I think I'll stick with Dr. Seuss, thanks."

"I suppose having kids is a good antidote to existential blight," Myriam muses. "Maybe some day I'll try it."

"I don't even know what you're talking about, existen... whatever. And I don't think I want to know." Amal turns around. "Benjamin! No, not the garbage!" she cries, as she bustles over to the two-year-old who is exploring the contents of the waste bin.

Maggie has been quietly slicing cucumbers. She feels like a young child, peering at the others from behind a screen or a curtain, listening to a private conversation. Unlike Amal, Maggie does want to know what Myriam is talking about. But she doesn't ask. She's afraid of drawing attention to herself, hovering there at the edge of that screen with her hands outstretched and nothing to say.

She's deep down in a hole again. A rope is being lowered, something she could grab hold of that could pull her up into the light. But it's not a physical act, grabbing hold, that's required. There's a password, a secret code that needs to be uttered, and Maggie has no idea what it is.

Jamila is kneading a mixture of lamb and bulghur, and watching Maggie steal glances at the three sisters as they converse. She has observed Maggie grow more comfortable in the months that she's been coming to their home. But today the young woman seems withdrawn again, a smile stationed on her thin lips but missing from her eyes; her shoulders more hunched over the cutting board.

"What about you, Maggie?" asks Myriam. "Do you like to read?"

"Um, kind of. I read a bit."

Myriam is looking at her expectantly.

"The last book I read was *The Diviners*." She doesn't say how long ago she read it.

"I loved that book," declares Leyla.

"Yeah, I liked it too." To her own ears, Maggie's voice sounds flat and insubstantial. As if she's reciting an entry in accounts receivable.

"The sex scenes were the pits, though," says Myriam. "The guy telling Morag to—" she pumps her pelvis back and forth, "—ride his stallion!"

"Myriam!" barks Jamila, and they all laugh.

"No, you wouldn't have liked those scenes, either, Mama," teases Leyla.

When Jamila first arrived in Canada, she felt cut adrift, all her landmarks vanished. Gone were the honey-brown hills, the smell of orange blossoms and frangipani flowers, the taste of figs and olives fresh from trees. They arrived in Toronto in November. Bitter wind lashed bare trees beneath a heavy sky. Along grey streets, grey-faced people hunched in bulky clothing. She couldn't get warm, felt as if all the blood in her had drained down into the sewers and out into the great grey lake that lay along the horizon. The bombed-out areas in Beirut she's been seeing lately on the television news remind her of her first impressions of Toronto: their neighbourhood seemed deserted. The inhabitants scuttled from houses into vehicles and back into houses again. Instead of the rich and varied tones of people in conversation, she heard only the low drone of distant traffic punctuated by the nearer sounds of it, car tires splishing on wet pavement, the diesel-rattle of trucks and buses gearing up or down.

Jamila knows what it is to be a foreigner, and alone. To be exiled from imperfect circumstances into incomprehensible ones, to feel a stranger in her own life.

That first year, she planted olive pits in pots, hoping some day to transplant them into their small yard. She bought a potted fig tree, visualizing it dripping with figs some day. Eventually she realized these things would never survive outside, but she nurtured the plants and added more so that eventually the foliage competed with the family for space in their house. Several years ago, they added a small solarium onto the south side of the house, and Jamila inhales the warm, damp greenness in there. It's not Mediterranean air, it's not the familiar breath of Lebanon. But it will do.

When Jamila looks at Maggie, she thinks of those early days in Canada. She thinks of a plant out of place, unable to thrive.

"Do you like plants, Maggie?"

"Um…"

Jamila puts a hand on Maggie's arm. "It's okay, you don't have to like them just because I do." She smiles. "For me, it's like they keep me alive. Not so much now, but before, in the first years after we arrived in Canada." The two women are in the small solarium adjacent to

Jamila's kitchen. "See this fig tree?"

"It's huge." Maggie gazes up through the canopy of the small tree, the sun pouring light into the leaves so they're glowing lime green.

"Eighteen years ago I bought it. I needed something like Lebanon here." Jamila fingers a branch, rubs a thumb gently across a leaf, removing dust. "Too bad it never rains inside, to clean the leaves." She and Maggie smile at each other.

Maggie inhales deeply. "Smells good in here."

"It's oxygen. Life. Especially in winter I need this smell." Jamila tilts her face up to the sun, closes her eyes a minute. "I was very lonely when we came from Lebanon. I thought it was a big mistake to come to this dead world. That is how it looked: all dead."

"It was winter?"

"Yes. November."

"No wonder. Was it better in the spring, the summer?"

Jamila tips her head to the left and then to the right. Leaf shadows play across her face as she moves. "It was not just the weather. There were no people."

Maggie frowns. "Weren't you in the city here?"

"Yes, a street like this one. People walk out of the house, get in the car, and drive away. End of the day, they go from car to house. Some days, they shovel the sidewalk or cut the grass, busy busy. Then go inside or drive away again. Even in stores, people are all business. Get what they need, then leave. Nobody stops to visit, spend time, talk."

Maggie is puzzled.

"In Lebanon? People everywhere talk, visit—in the street outside the house, in shops, everywhere. They take time, not rushing always, like here. In Canada, you need an appointment for visiting, put it on a calendar!" She shakes her head. "Even after I have been in Toronto so many years, I am still Lebanese in here." She places a hand on her chest. "So in our home, no appointments for visiting. You are always welcome here, like family."

Maggie flushes, smiles, squints up through the sunlight polishing every green leaf it touches.

After that day, Maggie usually wanders into the solarium when she's visiting. She doesn't know what many of the plants are—can't remember the names that Jamila has rhymed off—but she likes looking at the many textures and shades of green. The shiny fig tree, especially the bright emerald of the tender new leaves. The darker fern-type fronds of another plant. Cacti of all shapes and sizes, some as tall as she is. The pale, silver-green cascade from a hanging pot, necklaces strung with small fleshy crescents like miniature green bananas.

One Sunday when Maggie is preparing to go home after supper, Jamila takes her hand. "Come." She leads Maggie into the solarium and picks up a small potted cactus, a fleshy disk covered with prickles. "Maybe you would like it?" She holds the pot up between them. Maggie reaches tentatively for the plant, regarding Jamila with alarm.

"Don't worry! It won't bite you," Jamila laughs, and thrusts the pot into Maggie's hand. "Cactus is easy. If you forget to water, it survives. This one will surprise you with a bright orange flower one day."

"But what if I kill it?"

"So what? I will give you another."

Grace

WHEN GRACE AND KAIA JOINED ERIC at the Royal Arms late one Saturday afternoon, he was at a table with a small middle-aged woman they'd seen there before, sometimes sitting alone and always at the same table. The Royal Arms was a small barroom illuminated with industrial-style fluorescent lighting, lined with fake wood panelling and nicotine-tinted ceiling tiles. The wall across from the bar featured framed portraits of Queen Elizabeth and Prince Philip, separated by two crossed swords.

Eric waved Grace and Kaia over and introduced them to Pearl Adams. The first thing Grace noticed was how her eyes were just the opposite of her name: two shiny black stones. She was all compact angles, the half-hearted poof at the top of her short greying hair the only round thing about her. A small, sharp falcon's beak between high cheekbones. Her red lipstick emphasized the thinness of her lips. She held her mouth tight, as if it was clamped against what might come out of it.

"I met Pearl through my uncle, who just left," explained Eric. "Uncle Mike used to work with Pearl's husband. Her late husband," he added, glancing at Pearl.

She nodded. "Charlie."

"They used to come here together every Saturday, eh Pearl? She's been keeping up the tradition since Charlie passed away last year."

Pearl nodded again. It was an emphatic nod; she thrust her chin down once and then back up. "I come for my glass of beer every Saturday at four, just like we used to. Roger—the bartender—and the other regulars, it's like family. Specially after twenty years."

"That's a long time," said Kaia. "No wonder you keep coming."

Pearl lifted the glass of draft to her lips with both hands, using one palm to hold the bottom of the glass as she sipped. Grace leaned in to examine the older woman's hands.

"I've never seen hands like that before," she blurted.

Eric shot eye darts at Grace, then asked, "Bit of arthritis, I guess?"

Pearl snickered. "A bit." She held up her gnarled hands.

"Must be hard to do things," said Grace.

Pearl shrugged. "I manage. Charlie used to do a lot around the house, so it's harder now. This time of year it's the leaves I'm wondering about—it's not a big yard but there's lots of leaves down and I'm not one for raking."

"I love raking leaves!" exclaimed Grace.

Pearl looked at her.

"She's serious," groaned Eric. "It's one of those things about Grace."

"It's the smells in fall I love—that dead-leaf smell. Do you have poplars? They're the best." She inhaled deeply and exhaled with a loud sigh. "That earthy green smell, no wonder the beavers like them. I'll come rake your yard, just for the smell of it!"

Pearl's small living room was dim despite its windows, which were covered with shears and heavy drapes half drawn. Grace peered at photos on a side table. "Is this your wedding picture?"

Pearl's brief nod. "A good memory."

Another photo of a young woman with a baby. "Is this you?"

"It is. With our daughter, Theresa."

"Where is she now?"

"Out west—Calgary."

"Far away."

"Too far. She doesn't get home often; it costs too much."

"Is she an only child?"

"She is."

"Me too. What about you—do you have sisters and brothers?"

"I did." Pearl poured tea and Grace sat across from her. "Both my brothers already passed on."

"Died young I guess."

"They did. Anyway, we kind of got separated when I was young, after my father died."

"Oh? How old were you?"

"Not quite twelve. My mother and I came here where her sister was, but my brothers were old enough to be on their own, working. You know, bush work. We didn't see much of them. Then seems like we got one bit of bad news after the other, both of them only in their twenties when they died."

"That's tough."

"It is. Can't do anything about it, though. You just carry on."

Grace motioned toward a half-dozen dolls sitting along a shelf in the living room, each one neatly dressed, frills and lacy bits on collars and cuffs. "Do you collect dolls?"

"Just those ones. Some people start collecting and never stop, but after one shelf was full, that was enough for me. Just as well—the house was only big enough for Charlie and Theresa and me. Now it seems too big."

Grace nodded. "I collect a lot of stuff, so our house is pretty full by now."

"What do you collect?"

"Oh, different things. Mostly stuff I find outside—birds' nests, feathers, rocks, antlers, skulls. The skeleton of an owl I found dead one spring—you should see the talons on it! Shiny metallic black, this long"—she measured a couple inches between thumb and forefinger—"and sharp as razors. I don't think an owl could ever scratch an itch—it'd shred itself to bits!"

Pearl was startled into a laugh. "Well, I never heard of anybody collecting that kind of thing before. You know, dolls or spoons or plates, but dead birds—" she cackled.

"Spoons are in a drawer and plates are in a cupboard, but the really interesting stuff, like the owl skeleton, is out in the living room."

Pearl shook her head, grimacing.

"It makes me think about things, having that stuff around. What's in the world, how it all works." She shrugged and grinned.

Grace returned to Pearl's house periodically to help with chores, after which they usually shared a pot of tea. During one visit, Grace placed a very tiny white bone in the palm of Pearl's hand. It was only slightly larger than a round toothpick.

"It's from a sparrow. See how it's hollow?" Grace held it up so Pearl could peer down its short length. "For one thing, how can a bone that small be hollow and still be a bone—still form a skeleton, the thing that holds the bird together, lets it perch and hop and fly?"

"Why is it hollow?" asked Pearl, as she examined the little bone. "Where's the, the…bone marrow?"

"The marrow! I don't know! See? Just looking at this raises all kinds of questions. But it's hollow so the bird is light, so it can fly." Grace beamed at Pearl. "But: another question. If it's so light, how does it fly in a strong wind?"

Pearl frowned. "That's right—how?"

"I don't know. I have heard of migrating birds being blown off course in a storm, so a bird or a group of birds might show up in a place they usually don't belong."

"Do they find their way back?"

"Not sure—another thing to investigate! Lately, though, I've been reading about bigger animals—really big ones: elephants."

"I don't suppose you have part of a dead elephant in your house." Pearl's small mouth stretched into a thin grin.

"I wish! Wouldn't you love to see one up close—feel its thick, baggy skin, watch it move its pillar legs. They don't seem to have ankles; the cylinder of leg goes straight down to the ground and ends in a few toenails. But they actually hear through their feet! Sort of."

"Through their feet?"

"Wild, eh? Think of an elephant's big flat foot on the ground. It's like an ear—or a receiver, like a satellite dish. One elephant can call out, and the call is transferred into sound waves travelling through the ground. Other elephants *two kilometres* away can pick up the sound waves through their feet, and then the information goes up through their bones to their ears, where they can interpret the message. They can even tell who is sending it, if it's from an elephant they know. So through their feet, they can pick up a message, understand it, and know who sent it. Amazing!"

"What kinds of things would they be 'saying' to each other?"

"Maybe reporting danger, or a source of water or food. Or maybe even that an elephant has died—reporting the news, like a newspaper obituary, so other elephants can come and pay their respects."

Pearl scowled at what she thought was a tasteless joke.

"It's true! They seem to have funeral rituals—they've been seen standing around a dead elephant, kind of mourning it. In one case, a dead matriarch's calf seemed to be weeping and wailing while the other family members were making deep rumbling sounds. Then suddenly they all got really quiet, and then they started picking up dirt and leaves, and uprooting small trees, and placing them on the body. Like they were burying her. Then other groups of elephants would come along and stand over her body, swaying on their feet. Pretty amazing, eh?"

Pearl nodded slowly. "Very," she murmured. She was looking past Grace, toward the kitchen. "That's one thing we never had, was a funeral for my father."

"No?"

"No."

They were quiet a moment. Grace heard the fridge hum to life.

"No," said Pearl. "And anyway maybe you just don't have a funeral for somebody who's been hanged."

Grace gaped at her.

Pearl's curt nod. "My father was hanged for a murder he didn't commit."

"Whoa."

"They wouldn't believe my mother, that my father was home in bed the night Mean Oscar was killed. That's what us kids called him: Mean Oscar. He was a bad man. A dangerous man. It was drummed into my head to stay clear of him; he'd been up to no good with one of the girls. Lot of people in the town was happy to see him dead and gone. You'd think there'd be a long lineup of people wanting to shake the hand of the murderer, give him a medal instead of hanging him."

"How was he—Oscar—how was he killed?"

"Beaten to death. But my father was too small a man to take on that brute. Somebody else killed Oscar and let my daddy hang for it. It wouldn't happen like that today with DNA and all. Today they'd be able to prove he was innocent."

"Nobody knows who did it?"

"Nobody who's saying." She crossed her arms.

Grace couldn't take her eyes off Pearl. "Wow."

"I don't normally talk about this."

"I guess not."

"It was a long time ago. You carry on. Charlie and me, we had a good life together. I wish my daughter wasn't so far away, but there's things you can't change."

Maggie

"Maggie…"

Maggie glances up from her computer screen to see Jamila holding a small black case, her eyebrows raised in anticipation.

"It's lunch time! Are you ready?" Jamila smiles.

Maggie chuckles, pushes away from the desk. "Okay, okay. You just want to get me back for yesterday."

Jamila already has the case open on the corner of her desk and is arranging the backgammon pieces. "Yes! I taught you too well. Now you might be ready to play Amal, who is the Queen of Backgammon."

"Does she have time to play, with the kids? Maybe by now she's rusty and I'll have a chance against her too. Or maybe you just let me win yesterday."

"No, never," chides Jamila. "I like you, but not so much to give you victory."

The two women have shared the office since Maggie was hired, and they work well together, with a comfortable balance of conversation and silence. The lunchtime backgammon game has become part of their routine.

"Do you know Kahlil Gibran?" Jamila asks, frowning at the board.

"Gibran?"

"Kahlil Gibran. He is a Lebanese writer, poet, artist. One book is very popular: *The Prophet*."

"Maybe… I'm not sure."

"You might like it. He writes about life...work, love, suffering, happiness. Kind of poetry, kind of philosophy. Nice. I will lend it to you."

Maggie returns the book one Sunday at supper. When Leyla sees it, she exclaims, "*The Prophet*! I haven't read that for so long. It's good, isn't it—did you like it?"

"I did. Lots of good thoughts in it."

"Did you have a favourite part?" Leyla holds the book out to Maggie.

She takes the book. "Not sure if I can find it..."

While Maggie is searching, Leyla gets busy with supper preparations. "Is Amal coming?" she asks her mother. "What can I do?"

Jamila hands her two tomatoes. "The parsley too," she says, nodding toward the fridge.

"That's Maggie's job, that awful parsley—come on, Maggie."

But Maggie's still flipping pages. Then she says, "Here." She follows Leyla to the fridge, scanning the page while Leyla rummages around in it. Then she follows Leyla to the counter, the book open in her hands. "This part, about the soul unfolding itself like a lotus—it doesn't grow straight up like a reed; it's more like a lotus unfolding its countless petals." She looks up at Leyla, who is nodding and smiling.

"That is lovely—and so true," she says, then holds up a leafy green bundle. "The parsley with its countless leaves is waiting for your knife to make its countless cuts!"

≈

Leyla lends Maggie a book about Sufism. "If you like Gibran, I think you'll like the Sufis, too. Have you heard of the whirling dervishes?"

Maggie shakes her head.

"Mama, do you have that article, the pictures? These Sufis," she says to Maggie, "it's like a dance, but it's an ecstatic sort of thing—spiritual ecstasy—they whirl and whirl and spin like tops."

"Where—what part of the world are they in?"

"The Middle East, Iran… Sufism is a branch of Islam, a sort of mystical group. They have all kinds of little stories or parables that seem very simple on the surface but are really quite deep and philosophical."

"The men at the elephant, tell that one." Jamila turns to Maggie. "Maybe you heard it already?"

"I don't think so."

"So, there are six men, standing around an elephant, but they don't know it's an elephant because it's pitch dark out; they can't see. They are all feeling the part of the elephant where they're standing, trying to figure out what it is. The one by the ear says it's a fan, the one by the tail says it's a rope. The man feeling the leg thinks the thing is a pillar, and so on."

"They're all examining the same thing," says Maggie, "but each one sees it or interprets it differently."

"Because reality is subjective. Each person is limited in his or her experience of the whole, of reality. We think our view of something is the definitive one, when in fact we're just touching or seeing one aspect of it." Leyla sees something in Maggie's face, and grins. "That's what the Sufi stories are really good at. You read them, or hear them, and at first you can't exactly put your finger on what it is, but you see something—or something opens up. Like the sun just coming up over the horizon, then maybe it disappears into a cloud, but there's been a brief illumination. And the more and more you encounter these stories, the clearer things get."

"Why did you study law, instead of, say, philosophy?"

"I did study philosophy in undergrad. Logic, ethics, questions about existence and meaning. The legal clinic law I practise is mostly about human rights. Providing legal services to underprivileged people. Refugee claims, for example. I sort of think of that kind of law as a practical application of philosophy. The Sufis say you don't have to divorce yourself or cloister yourself from 'normal' life to be a Sufi. You just live Sufism. Not that I'm a Sufi by any means! But Sufism aims at a developed consciousness—becoming more conscious beings. I was searching for something I could do that felt like there would be a net benefit or contribution to society rather than a net subtraction or depletion. I think there's far too much emphasis on materialism and consumerism in this society—having all this *stuff*—the planet can't sustain that kind of consumption, and I think it depletes us as people. So I didn't want to work in a field that supported the making and selling of all that stuff. I wanted to be useful to people in a helpful way, but I could never be a social worker or a doctor. With law I can help people without getting embroiled in the messy bits—the biological and psychological pathologies."

"So…what do you think about your father's business, then—buying and selling imported *stuff*?"

Jamila regards Leyla with raised eyebrows. "This is a good question!"

"See where all this talk leads—now I am in trouble!" laughs Leyla. "But I've learned not to try to tell my father how to live. He knows better than to listen to me, eh Mama! What I was talking about was choosing how to live my own life. That's all."

"You see," Jamila says to Maggie. "She makes a good lawyer—knows when to keep her mouth closed."

Eventually, Leyla lends Maggie a book about the Chinese sage Lao Tzu. "*Being* rather than *doing*, that's one of the things I took from it," says Leyla.

Maggie squints at her. "Being rather than doing?"

"Instead of focussing always on *doing* this and *accomplishing* that, the important thing is just to *be*."

"To be."

"Or not to be!" laughs Leyla. "That is the question."

"Oh God," groans Amal, as she sets the table. "Now we're into the Shakespeare. Look what you've started, Maggie. Good thing Myriam's not here or she'd be strutting around dramatizing the whole thing."

"She does love the Bard," says Leyla. "He's what led her into graduate work in literature, I'm sure."

"When will she be home next?" asks Maggie.

"Soon, I hope!" exclaims Jamila. "She is too far away. Why BC when she can study here in Toronto?"

"That's just Myriam," shrugs Amal. "She likes to spread her wings. She likely won't get home again before Christmas."

"Six months from now—too long!" declares her mother.

"Yes, your baby has flown the nest, Mama. But lucky for you, Leyla and I are home-bodies. We don't stray far. What about you, Maggie—your home town is pretty far away. You never go back to visit?"

Maggie shakes her head.

"Tell me again where you're from?" asks Amal's husband, Rob. "Up north somewhere, near Lake Superior?"

"Yeah. Barret River. Up past Sault Ste. Marie."

"It's supposed to be gorgeous up there. A friend of mine drove to Thunder Bay last year and couldn't stop talking about the rugged shore, the huge, clear lake. You don't miss it?"

"Um, well, not really. I didn't spend much time at the lake. The town is inland a bit. Just a dumpy little town, really."

By now they are all sitting at the table. Jamila is passing platters of food around. "There is lots—eat, eat! You know what we Lebanese say: the eating is proportionate to the love!"

"What's at Barret River," Rob wants to know. "Why is there a town there—forestry or something?"

"A big pulp and paper mill, and gold mines in the area too."

"Did your father work at the paper mill, or—?"

"Yeah, the mill."

"When were you there last?"

"About fifteen years ago."

"That's a long time!" exclaims Rob. "You haven't been back to visit... since your parents died? You haven't wanted to go back?"

"No reason to."

Grace

GRACE SPENDS SO MUCH TIME THINKING and talking about animals and birds that Eric once teased that she cares more about them than about her own species. But really she cares about people the same way she does the woodpeckers and dolphins, the ants, the bees, and everything: what would life be like without all these creatures? Pretty boring. But not just that. Pretty...empty. Because she's human, she's happy to have other humans around; she wouldn't want to be the only person on earth. That's why Noah took two of everything on the boat.

Well it's true the story says God *told* Noah to take two of everything: those were his instructions. Which shows that God knew a thing or two about biology and maybe even psychology. She has wondered about God, and Jesus and the Holy Spirit—what they talked about in church. Grace liked church as a kid; it was always lively with the singing and people shouting things out and chanting in strange languages and sometimes falling down. And it was never the same routine, like at the Humphries' church: everybody standing up and sitting down at the same time, everybody saying the same words in response to the minister's words, and every Sunday the same like that. At her own church, she'd join in the singing, loudly and always off-key, and when people were invited up to the front, she'd go too, so she could see what was happening. She herself never fell down or spoke in tongues, but she was intrigued when others did. Her mother always stayed at her seat, though; she never joined the circle at the front. She'd sing a bit, but generally was quieter than lots of the other people there. Grace never heard her mother shout out a halleluiah, for instance. In fact, Grace wasn't sure why she insisted they go to church every Sunday except for the fact that her mother got to see her friends there.

But the Holy Spirit and God: it's hard to figure out how they're the same. The Holy Spirit being the thing that seemed to rush through people, the mighty wind the pastor would talk about. That wind filling people up so much they couldn't contain it and it just babbled out of them. Sort of like the experience of standing on the rocks at the edge of the lake, facing out where sky and water meet, the horizon dissolving and other boundaries too, like the boundary of skin, so there's nothing to separate you from the Everything around you. That must be something like the Holy Spirit: the thing you might draw in with a breath, something that stealthy.

The God bit is harder to fathom, though, at least the one they talked about at church. That one was all about boundaries and rules; that one had a temper. He talked about love and salvation but you got the sense he'd be more inclined to break down your door than sneak in through your pores.

But it doesn't matter anyway. It's possible to listen for the voice of the Holy Spirit, and hear it everywhere. To stand beneath the wide sky and listen, and hear not just one thing, but many.

And there's no point in worrying too much about the details.

Maggie

"WHAT ARE YOU GOING TO DO WITH YOUR LIFE, MAGGIE?" Jamila is hunched over the backgammon board.

"I thought I was doing something already. I'm working at Haddad Enterprises, I'm …" She pauses. Then smiles. "Are you starting to nag me about getting married and having kids?"

"No, not that. Maybe later, but not now, not until you first find where you are going."

"Why do I have to be going somewhere? I'm here. Or is Fareed planning to fire me?"

"No, no; Fareed will never fire you. You have to choose on your own to go."

"I like it here. Why would I go?"

"There is more for you than this office. I see more."

Maggie leans back in her chair and sighs. "I don't see it."

"Why don't you go back to school? Go to university. You can do anything you want, become a lawyer, a teacher." She leans forward when Maggie starts laughing. "Really, you can. This, here—this is a dead end for you."

"We could change my title, make me Chief Financial Officer of Haddad Enterprises; that's not bad," she says, smiling, trying to get Jamila to lighten up. "That sounds pretty professional."

"It's not just the title; you know that. There is something else you are supposed to do."

Maggie rolls her eyes.

"You are like my daughters—their eyes go to the ceiling like that when I tell them what I think they should do."

"But you're not that kind of mother—always bossing them around? You're good with them, you have a good relationship."

"Now, yes. But earlier, not so good. The teenage years—you know. We had many fights, especially Leyla."

"Really? What kind of fights—yelling and screaming?"

"Much yelling. I tried to make Leyla stay home but she went out anyway—staying late with her friends, drinking, smoking marijuana. She said, *Hashish comes from Lebanon, I am just being Lebanese!*" Jamila shakes her head. "Those were bad days."

"But she turned out fine—they all did."

"Yes, lucky."

"Not just luck. You're a good mother. And Fareed, too—you're good parents."

"Thank you. We try. And what about you, Maggie; were you a bad teenager?"

"Yeah, the same."

"And your mother, what did she do?"

"The same as you, but worse."

Jamila shrugs. "She was probably trying too, like Fareed and me." Then she asks softly, "Did things get better before she died?"

Maggie scratches her neck. "No, not really."

"You don't like to talk about her, or your father…it makes you sad."

"Yeah."

"Sometimes it's better to talk, though. It can make you feel…" her hands stir up the air around her, "lighter."

Maggie looks out the window. "Actually, talking about them makes me feel worse." Her voice a taut wire.

"Ah. It's hard."

Maggie nods.

"Maybe sometime it will be easier." Jamila touches Maggie's arm.

"Anyway, you have our family now. And that is why," she says, her voice brightening, "I am telling you about going to school. The same as I would say to one of my own daughters. It's true! I watch you and Leyla talking. You like to talk about things—ideas, philosophy. You want to learn more. You should go to university."

"I don't know…"

"It's possible for you. You can do it. Go to university; study what you want."

Maggie is quiet for a minute. Then in a small voice she says, "But I don't know what I want."

"It's okay, not knowing."

"It doesn't really feel okay."

Jamila waits.

"It feels stupid."

Jamila leans forward, looks Maggie in the eye. "You are not stupid. You are searching. Like Kahlil Gibran talks about. Searching is not stupid; it is just life."

Maggie is startled to find herself crying. But Jamila is less surprised. She goes to Maggie and puts her arms around her. Cradled there, her head against Jamila's chest, Maggie empties herself of tears.

It takes a long time, but Jamila doesn't let go of her until she's done.

≈

Maggie can't believe she's been talked into this. She's thirty-three years old in a lecture theatre filled with nineteen-year-olds. She feels like a grandmother. And also like a fraud: what right does she have to be here?

After working all day, she has difficulty staying awake during the three-hour lecture one night a week. The course also involves occasional laboratory sessions, which are presided over by a teaching assistant named Larry. He's a pale fellow Maggie's age who, during the second lab, is accompanied by a white rat. All through the session,

Larry holds the rat, stroking it, as he discusses scientific methodology. He's uneasy addressing the students, barely looks up at them. After an excruciating hour, as everybody packs up their books and stumbles out the door, Larry approaches Maggie.

The rat ambles up his arm to his shoulder. With one hand he gently guides it to the other shoulder, and it wanders down that arm. "Good to see a mature student here among the youngsters." He and the rat repeat their routine, as if Larry is a human hamster wheel. "You did a good job on that first lab report."

Maggie grimaces. "Thanks." She can't take her eyes off the rat.

Not one for eye contact himself, he directs his gaze around Maggie's throat, her left ear. "Want to hold it?"

She takes a step back, shaking her head.

Larry laughs. "He doesn't bite."

"That's okay."

"So are you majoring in psych?"

"Not sure—I'm only taking the one course now. I'm still working full time, just trying this out."

"You should major in it. Experimental psychology is especially interesting." Larry has the rat in one palm now, and is stroking its head with a finger. "Rats are intriguing creatures—very smart. We learn a lot about human behaviour by studying rats." His eyes are on Maggie's chest now. "Would you like to see the housing room?"

"The housing room?"

"The place where we keep the rats—where we house them."

"Uh, I don't think so—not tonight. I have to get going. Work in the morning. But thanks."

He places the rat in the crook of an elbow and cradles it there. "Sure, another time maybe."

"The psych department psycho," sputters Amal. "That guy belongs in an Alfred Hitchcock movie."

Fareed shakes his head. "You see?" he says to Jamila. "Look where this goes, this big idea of yours, Maggie going to university." He turns to Maggie. "What are you going to learn from a bunch of crazy people?"

"Never mind, he is just one—not even the professor. What about the rest, your lectures," entreats Jamila. "Tell us something interesting, what you learn." Her eyes are all hope.

"Uhh…"

"Well, you are just starting. Give it time."

Grace

THERE HAS JUST BEEN A PIECE ON THE RADIO SHOW *Quirks and Quarks*, about social behaviour in ant colonies. A researcher said that ants will warn each other if they have an infection—by knocking their knees together! She laughs aloud, sits back in the chair and knocks her knees a few times. "Stay away! It might be bubonic plague!" Those ants, honestly. So clever. What if humans could do that, send specific messages by knocking our knees or elbows together. It's true we do communicate with gestures, but we have voices also, unlike the ants. We rely much more on words than on gestures.

Or do we? We think they're reliable, but sometimes words conflict with what the body proclaims loud and clear. The look of alarm on Tina Parker's face when she sees Grace coming—the way her eyes seem to draw into her head and then dart left and right. The way her gait changes: she almost stops, but then she seems to make up her mind about something and walks even faster as she approaches. A painful smile splits Tina's lips as she trots out the words she's been rehearsing: *Oh, hi Grace, good to see you.* Tinsel. Or radio static. Grace knows what frequency Tina's on and it's not the words themselves that tell her.

Tina's not that interested in ants or amphibians. In fact, not many people are. Most people don't seem interested in very many things, actually. Grace sighs. Other than Kaia and Eric. And then there's Bart, who spends most of his time doing research at the library where she works. Grace and he like to tell each other about the new things they learn; it's incredible with the Internet how much you can discover.

Bart's a retired police officer with a square reddish face and a silver brush cut. He's a history buff, especially keen on genealogy. "There's so much history tied up in a family—think of everything your ancestors have seen," he said recently. "Where they lived, how they lived—all of that reflects the development of communities and even the whole country. In fact, families are a microcosm of the history of the world!"

He was incredulous that Grace had so little information about her own ancestors. "You don't know anything about them—not even your grandparents?"

"Not really. I couldn't get much out of my mother about her family. And my father died before I was born, so it was hard to find out anything from him! All I know is he was from a small place called Drayton."

Bart got so enthused when he heard that, he just about knocked over the microfiche machine. "Drayton! You mean over by Chapleau?"

"Yeah, I think so. Have you heard of it?"

"Yes! I've been reading a book about ghost towns in Northern Ontario—not places with real ghosts, but abandoned towns, mostly places with sawmills that ran for awhile and then shut down."

"My grandfather worked at the sawmill in Drayton. Does the book talk about it?"

"A bit about the mill, but it's mostly stories about goings-on in the town. A murder. Another guy who died by falling into a bonfire."

"How on earth does that happen?"

"Who knows," shrugged Bart. "It's just one of those crazy stories. There were a couple hundred people living in Drayton at one time but you'd never know it now. The buildings are all gone."

"There's nothing left?"

"Doesn't sound like it."

"We'd find something if we looked. Like with the dinosaurs: now the only sign of them is the fossils they find in the ground. There's probably stuff lying around there from those days, lots of it just buried."

Henry

ON A WALL IN THE SCHOOLHOUSE IS A LARGE MAP of Northern Ontario. There's a lot of blue on it: lakes everywhere, all shapes and sizes. Henry places a finger on the one near Drayton, his home. It's one of the larger lakes, and from it a river runs north all the way to James Bay. He traces the river with his finger, through two hundred miles of boreal forest and muskeg, all the way to the salty sea. But just a mile downstream from the lake is where he is, in a village nestled in the curve of the river that runs along to the south and west of the townsite. On the north the town is bordered by the railway. The river and the railway are why the town is here: jack pine and spruce are cut all along the lake and driven the short distance downstream to the sawmill established by the Drayton Lumber Company in the late 1920s. The lumber is then transported out by train. Operations were suspended during the Depression but resumed in the early '40s, and gradually the town has grown to a population of almost two hundred people.

Along the river near the railway is the mill yard with its various buildings—the sawmill itself, the horse barn and blacksmith shop, the machine shop, a couple of warehouses and sheds. At the edge of the mill yard are the company office, a cookhouse, and two bunkhouses for single employees. The main townsite is organized in a neat grid pattern, with one main axis road running parallel to the tracks and two shorter roads intersecting the main road at right angles.

The town becomes ragged around the periphery, though, with log cabins and clapboard houses and shacks scattered at the edge of

155

the clearing and into the woods toward the river. Some of these are occupied by mill employees who brought their wives and children here before the company built housing for families. Other dwellings in this part of town house people who engage in a mixture of subsistence and wage activities, as hunters, trappers, prospectors, and itinerant workers for the logging company or the railway. A couple of these families, like Henry's, have a few pigs and chickens scrabbling in the dirt. Shanghai Dick's place is on the edge of town and serves as the unofficial pub and gaming house: his moonshine is cheaper than booze brought in on the train from Capreol. There's not much else to do for entertainment in the late 1940s in Drayton.

≈

August sun warms the cool morning, burning silver mist off the lake. An osprey hovers high above the water, just out from shore. It dips and rises, tipping its wings one way and then another in the sunlight. Suddenly it drops like a stone into the water, crashing through the mirrored surface and then rising up through the shattered light with a fish in its talons. Henry watches it disappear into tree shadows before he collects the minnows from the trap he'd set out the day before.

It's Sunday, the family's fishing day, the day his patience is always tested: his father is never able to wake up early enough for Henry's liking, dragging his solvent-smelling body from the bed near noon, his red eyes like warning beacons, scattering the boys into the yard.

Eventually a lunch is packed, fishing gear gathered, and the canoe launched into the lake's afternoon choppiness. Henry, eleven years old, takes the bow and his father the stern. Nine-year-old Frank and their mother sit between them, in the bottom of the canoe. Henry's father's mood improves as he pauses in his paddling to swig from the flask he keeps in his pocket. He begins to sing old Voyageur songs and doesn't mind when his two sons shush him once the minnows are on the hooks and the lines dropped into the water. And when Henry pulls up the first pickerel, he's helpless against his father's enthusiasm and praise.

"That's my boy, my first born son. You're more of a man than any of us here, including your mother." He gives his wife a tender push on the shoulder. "Show me that fish, Henry; are we ready for a shore lunch yet or do we need the good Lord to come down and multiply it for the masses? Oh, it's a brute! But let's see who gets the next one—maybe it'll even be you, Mother." As he leans forward to give her a kiss, he rocks the canoe and they all shout at him to settle down. He grins and sighs as he pulls the bottle from his pocket again.

One Sunday, casting from shore, Henry's father's reckless hook snags the flesh on Henry's arm. He sobers enough to remove the hook, soaking the wound generously with the alcohol in his flask. Then he implores Henry to take a drink, to fortify his constitution to overcome the trauma. As Henry raises the flask to his mouth, he thinks he might gag from the hot jagged smell of the whiskey, but he is not going to let this moment go. The expression on his father's face—a mixture of collusion and sloppy pride—braces Henry to swallow a searing mouthful of the alcohol with minimal sputtering. For a moment, Henry is in his father's world, not merely by default, but by invitation. Henry feels his father is looking at him for the first time, searching for recognition. And most amazing of all, for both of them: finding it.

≈

They reach the edge of a pond skimmed with ice and glittering snow, and flanked by dead spruce and cedars, grey ghosts stranded in the frozen wetland. Henry and Mort stop and look across. A woodpecker hammers a tree, splintering the silence. They hear the wingbeats of two ravens flying low overhead, one pursuing the other. The first one rolls over as the second one approaches it. They take turns doing this, chasing and rolling in mid-air, calling to each other with strangled squawks or a series of hollow pops, like marbles being dropped into a metal cup.

Mort rubs his jaw, the nails on his thick fingers rough and cracked. He has sandy-grey eyebrows that look as if a bird or mouse might nest in them. Blue eyes with long pale lashes: an unexpected softness in the ruddy, grey-stubbled face. His voice is also at odds with his physical presence: higher than one would expect; thin but raspy.

"Funny birds, ravens. Real playful."

The boy nods.

They head into the bush to check a marten trap they set the day before at the base of a large birch tree. After a short distance, Mort stops and indicates wolf tracks veering onto the trail that's been dusted with snow. "Pretty fresh," he says, peering through the trees ahead of them. As they round a bend in the trail, they see the wolf further down the path, walking nose to the ground. Suddenly it stops, raises its head and sniffs toward the left, in the direction of the tree where Mort set the trap. The wolf takes a step off the trail in that direction, then stops, sensing the air with its entire body—nose, ears, eyes, and every strand of fur. It changes its mind and turns back onto the trail, walks ahead several feet to a log that angles back from the trail a short distance toward the birch tree. It walks along the top of the log, and when it reaches the end, it gingerly paws the ground before stepping down. It continues doing that, raking through snow and leaves with its front paw as it makes its way from the log to the marten caught in the leg-hold trap. The wolf quickly severs the trapped leg of the marten, grabs the animal in its jaws, and returns along the path it cleared. Then it lopes down Mort's trail until it's out of sight.

Mort starts to raise his rifle when the wolf is making its way along the fallen log, but when he realizes it's checking the ground for traps, he lowers the gun. He and Henry stand in the snow, barely breathing, watching the wolf steal the marten. After it runs off, Mort looks at Henry. "Smart fella; I guess he deserves a free lunch."

Morton is not a loquacious man; he isn't given to gossip or grand tales about his bush work. He was married long ago to a woman who died in childbirth: a first child who also died. Mort was helpless in that situation, unable to ease his wife's pain or stop her bleeding, to save her or the boy baby. His skill in the bush is for him a kind of compensation, a means of addressing death as something inevitable, consciously acknowledged. He recognizes his role as a trapper: he is responsible for individual deaths, not for the great cycle of life and death. With each animal he traps and skins, he recognizes a death is in his hands, regarding it with a mixture of fatalism and regret: every living thing must die, whether it starves or is preyed upon this winter or is claimed eventually by old age or disease.

When eight-year-old Henry started showing up at Mort's cabin on the edge of town, the old man began to include the boy in his daily activities. One time early on, he had a fire going outside to steam the long strips of black ash for snowshoe frames. After Mort used the long poker stick to expose bright coals, he suggested to Henry, "That looks like a good spot there for another log; how 'bout you put one on there?" When Henry didn't quite get the log in the right place, Mort handed the poker to the boy so he could push the wood nearer its destination. "Every fire needs a poke now and then," said Mort.

With the old man, Henry was attentive and observant. He mirrored Mort's patience and copied his techniques for sharpening knives and tying knots, starting a fire, whittling sticks to a fine point. Around his father, though, Henry was all thumbs, dropping things, missing nails with the hammer, cutting kindling too thick or too thin. He'd summon his father's impatience with his fumbling. But Mort never raised his voice or grabbed a tool from the boy's hand, or shoved him away like his father did. He never called him stupid or clumsy. He gave Henry minimal guidance and rewarded him with adult talk about the days ahead, the tasks that needed doing, whatever the season was right for.

When Henry was ten, the old man took him trapping for the first time, showed him how to set rabbit snares and traps for beaver, otter, marten, fox. Taught him how to separate the beaver fur from the fatty layer underneath, stretch the furs on willow frames and scrape the remaining bits of fat and flesh off the hides. They went partridge hunting together, Henry initially using a slingshot, until Mort taught him how to load, aim, and fire the shotgun.

Henry's father barely tasted the partridge and rabbit meat in the stews he gulped down at supper before heading off to play poker at Shanghai Dick's.

≈

There's snow in all the trees; white veils of it fall from the branches Henry brushes against as he makes his way along the portage trail to the lake. It snowed in the night but today it's clear in the way only a winter sky can be clear. The March sun casts shorter shadows, filters down from above the trees rather than slanting sideways through them. Chickadees flit through the branches, unaware of their hollow-boned frailness. Their cheery *deedeedee* the only sound other than the whump and squeak of the snowshoes beneath Henry's feet. The crisp air is singed with the faint smell of hot sawdust from the mill.

He's supposed to be crammed inside the one-room schoolhouse with the other dozen kids from the town. But he hates being there. Everything about the school seems small to Henry. He's tall and strong for fourteen, and always feels jammed into the desks that are lined up from wall to wall with barely an aisle in between. The large wooden teacher's desk fills the small space at the front of the room between the rows of students and the blackboard. The shelves and cupboards of books and school supplies, even the things that would normally interest him—models of dinosaur skeletons, the microscope and the globe, the beaver skull with its two long orange teeth—all of it is just clutter that seems to crowd up against him, niggle and natter at his brain instead of stimulating it. He'd rather be outside splitting firewood or feeding the chickens and pigs, or helping Mort make rawhide. After they'd scraped the flesh off a moose hide, Mort showed Henry how soaking it in a mixture of water and wood ash made it easier to remove the fur. "Got to get all that off so it don't rot the hide," Mort explained; then he added, chuckling, "D'ya learn that kind of chemistry in school?"

Henry's younger brother Frank doesn't mind going to school because it means getting away with fewer chores. Frank hates scrounging firewood from the bush, dragging home deadfalls and armloads of brittle branches snapped off the trunks of jack pine and spruce. He hates helping their mother with the laundry—although Henry hates that too. Gripping one end of each item of clothing while his mother or brother twists the other end, wringing out the wash water and then the rinse water. In the summer they do this outside, the blackflies and mosquitoes making them want to murder each other. In the winter, the washing is hung on ropes strung along behind the cookstove and across the edge of the kitchen, darkening the window. The smell of steaming wool and clammy cotton fills the house, along with whiffs of smoke from the fire that needs constant stoking. The interior panes of their windows are often feathered with frost on cold winter days. This morning Henry pressed a finger against the white etchings and felt them melt beneath his skin, felt his finger being drawn through the frost to the clear glass pane. With one eye he peered through that opening, saw the low sun burn a hole through the trees and set alight a swath of snow on the purple ground. That's when he decided to skip school and do something useful instead.

When he arrives at the lake, he walks out onto the ice a short distance and puts down his fishing gear. The lake is so long that Henry has never been to the far end of it, and here it's wide as well, a vast expanse of glittering snow beneath the blue arc of sky. Sunlight somersaults around him: a bounding, boundless light. Impossible that so much energy resides in the midst of such silence. A slight breeze cuffs him on the cheek, teases water from his eyes. As if the sky is signalling that it knows he's here, it's picked up his scent, has him in its sights. He exhales slowly, watching his pale breath waver in the air and then disappear. Something large but tentative is stirring in his chest, pushing against it from the inside, as if he's inhaled too much cold air and there's a well of it in there, deep and aching. It's something like wonder: the fact of him being here, the fact of him being. He's small beneath the sky: a dark speck on the ice, a snow flea—and yet as irrefutable and luminous as those trees on shore, the bold bright birches reaching up, startling the blue.

He begins to chisel a hole in the ice. Bright shards fly up, catch on his clothes. When he stops to rest, the silence is thunderous after the noise of the blade and his heavy breath. He resumes chiselling until he's through to the dark water below, then squats and removes a mitt, scoops chunks of ice and slush from the hole. He drops his line into it and waits for a trout to latch on. It's hard to imagine living things down there, carrying on, oblivious to the still, dead cold of winter. The black opening in the ice is like a magician's hat, out of which he'll pull something unexpected and alive, twisting and muscular, shimmering silver in the sunlight. Then he'll kneel, and while bracing the fish against the ice, he'll put two fingers in its mouth and give the head a swift upward jerk, snapping its spine.

≈

The ground is wet with rain. A single light standard outside the warehouse casts a gauzy light onto the dirt below. Just beyond it, the dark shape of an animal, back hunched, breath coming out in grunts. It's caught something, it's making a meal of its prey. Then it stands. Two-legged. Wobbly. The cone of dull light catches it: the tweed cap and the face beneath it, the staggering boots, calf-high, pants tucked in. The shape of his father lurching into the deeper dark. No other sound but the drip-drip of rain from the roof of the warehouse, and a clanging in the boy's head, like someone striking a heavy iron bell with a crowbar.

Henry must have fallen asleep sometime in the night, though he didn't expect to. Wakes to the sound of wood being thumped into the stove, the squeak and clang of the heavy fire door opening and closing. Immediately a panic is there, thrumming through him like the sound of a distant train. What did he see by the warehouse? Then a momentary sweet pause: it was a dream. Or not a dream but nothing serious, his father having fallen down while out on a drunken ramble. But that train keeps rumbling toward him, louder and louder, insisting on something else.

It's not quite dawn, murky light leaking in around the dark trees outside. He can hear his parents' voices in the kitchen: his father's slurred impatience, his mother's anger. Water being poured into a pot. They're arguing about butchering a pig.

"It's not even daylight," she's saying.

"Shut your fuckin' yap; I'm doing it now."

"When the boys are up they can help you—why now?"

"I said, Shut. Your. Fuckin'. Yap." The door slamming.

By the time Henry and his brother get outside, the ground is black with blood beneath the pig hanging by its feet from the horizontal pole set up on the butchering ground. Henry can barely look at his father, at his blood-spattered boots and clothes.

No witnesses, the court is told. But a motive, some kind of evidence. Enough to sentence a man to hang for beating Oscar Saari to death. His father grunts when he hears the news, turns and walks out of the kitchen.

The boy saw the police take Lazarus Dumont away, hands cuffed behind his back, the trapped animal look in his eyes, a look that said No. No. No.

Inside the boy's head, inside his chest, the bell being struck again and again.

≈

"I need your son's help," Mort tells Henry's mother. "Time to get the traps out. Can I have the boy for a few days?"

Mort has seen Henry only once, briefly, in the weeks since the warehouse incident. Henry's absence alone was notable, but when Mort saw him, he knew something was wrong. Something feral in Henry's eyes, the look of an animal caught in a leg-hold trap, still alive. In the case of a wolf or a fox, Mort knows what to do: fire a clean shot into the head, killing the animal instantly. But Mort doesn't know what has got hold of Henry, though he guesses it's more than he himself ever dealt with at the age of fourteen.

Henry has never been afraid in Mort's company before. But now he is uneasy with the old man: afraid that Mort might read something in his face the way he reads the almost invisible animal trails through the bush.

Mort is familiar with camouflage, the way various creatures can make themselves invisible, like the striped bittern in the wetland pointing its long, slender beak into the air so it will be indecipherable from the sedges. He observes the boy's silence, more pronounced than usual. But he doesn't press him. He makes excuses to stay out longer than a few days at his tiny trapline cabin, suggests the need to investigate streams and ponds they normally don't visit. As if the demon haunting Henry might ease its grip if they stay out there long enough.

But it's the wrong time of year for the bush to have that effect, to lighten the load Henry is dragging. November's weary sky is too heavy, and even the season's first snow seems to enhance the gloom rather than brighten it; it only prolongs the slow, eerie light of dusk. And for the first time, Henry seems bruised by the animal deaths, reluctant to peel the hare's fur from the slender body as if turning the animal inside out, and reluctant to eviscerate it as Mort has taught him. Mort can see the boy's hesitation, but he doesn't take the knife from him. He reasons that Henry has to carve through whatever has gotten hold of him, flay it open, clean it out.

Eventually, thanks to Morton's own silence, Henry begins to trust himself in the old man's company again. His hand on the knife regains its steadiness, though his eyes have a new look about them, like the dull film across the eyes of a snowshoe hare strangled by a thin wire snare.

≈

Henry's been out working in the bush all winter, staying in the camp with the rest of the crew. He isn't felling trees yet; he's too green, the men tell him. He helps with the limbing once the trees are down.

It's a large spruce that does it. Henry hears the crack and the shout, looks over and sees Cyprien Proulx turn his head too late. For Cyprien there's not enough time; for Henry, there's too much— enough to watch the man crumple beneath the massive trunk.

It's near the end of the cutting season. Cyprien has been talking about getting the hell out of Drayton, getting on that train, maybe never coming back. Henry tastes Cyprien's words on his own tongue: not the bitterness he expects, but something else.

He finds Mort sitting in front of his cabin on a low chair he'd made from scraps of lumber, his legs extended out in front of him. A mug of tea rests on his thigh. The ground is wet, most of the snow gone now but for patches in the shade.

"Tea on the stove," says Mort.

Henry goes into the cabin and returns with a mug, sits on the block of wood Mort uses as a chopping block.

"Bad news about the Proulx fella."

Henry looks up into the crown of the birch tree, a hint of burgundy in the small branches outlined against the blue sky.

After a few minutes, Mort says, "Happens more often than we'd like it to, an accident like that."

Henry nods.

Two squirrels dart past them on the ground. One chases the other in a spiral up a spruce tree, bits of bark flying, the high-pitched staccato of its chatter continuing even after the interloper has disappeared.

"So what'll you do now then? Work at the mill?"

"Maybe. My old man is working there for the summer again. I might too."

Mort swirls the tea around in the mug, takes a swig. Empties the last drops of it onto the ground. "They're always lookin' for section hands on the railway."

"Yeah." A moment later, "I don't know."

"You planning to move on?" Mort is leaning back with his eyes closed, face turned up to the sun. Shadows from the naked birch branches cast a net on the ground beside him.

Henry looks at Mort's large hands clasped across his belly, the brown-tinged burn holes studding his red wool jacket. It's done up crooked, one side of the collar higher than the other. He looks at Mort's face, attentive as a wolf even with his eyes closed.

He'd be leaving the old man behind.

Grace

GRACE HAS JUST BEEN TELLING PEARL ABOUT HER FRIEND Bart at the library—about his interest in genealogy. "I've never looked into all that," she says, "but I do wonder about my father, and my grandparents on both sides. I don't know anything about them."

"Your mother never told you anything?"

"She never wanted to talk about them."

"Some things are better forgotten."

"Bart was telling me there's a book that mentions the town my father was from—about things that went on there and in other small towns around the north. He's going to lend it to me."

Pearl is taking two mugs from the cupboard above the kitchen counter. "You know where your father was from at least?"

"That's the only thing I know about him. A small place called Drayton, somewhere—"

One of the mugs hits the counter with a startling bang. Pearl has dropped it, and stands staring at Grace.

"What's—"

"Drayton? Did you say Drayton?"

"Yeah—what—"

Pearl is shaking her head, chuckling weakly. "Well, I never." She studies Grace. "A funny thing to know someone who's even heard of Drayton, let alone have a father from there."

Grace frowns. "You ...?"

"That was my town."

"You? Drayton? That's where—your father—Drayton?!"

"That's right."

"Wow! That's amazing—what a small world! You—maybe you knew my father, maybe you're the same age, I don't know—did you know him?"

"What was his name?"

"Hal White."

Pearl squints, searching her memory. "Hal White…. I don't recall a Hal. Did he have brothers, sisters?"

"I don't know."

Pearl looks up at the ceiling, then suddenly back at Grace. "The Whites. Frank was more my age, and his older brother…*Henry*, that's it."

"He was called Henry? You knew him?"

"It was a long time ago, but yes. Weren't many kids there in Drayton."

"What was he like? Do you remember?"

Pearl thinks. "We were all just kids. I can't say what anybody was like."

"So Frank was more your age—do you know what happened to him?"

Pearl shakes her head. "I was only eleven or twelve when we left. Can't say what happened to anybody."

Maggie

SOMETHING LIKE YARN OR HEAVY THREAD IS HANGING out of her mouth. She pulls it and it keeps coming; she can feel it unravelling in her stomach. She wants scissors, wants to cut this freakish thing before someone sees. Then suddenly she flattens out, like a flag, and she's flying: a kite, rainbow-shimmering and gorgeous, soaring through the sky, the long string still there but not unravelling now; it's anchored somewhere inside her. She's not sure where the other end of the string is—whether someone has hold of it or not, and she doesn't care. She wakes from this dream smiling, wanting to re-enter it.

Iris

GRACE WAS BORN IN THE SPRING. Her second name Margaret, to connect the two of them. And though she didn't exactly bend to my will, she didn't resist with her sister's vehemence. She was more like a river that parts around a boulder in its path and continues on its merry way, lapping up the sun.

She was forever bringing things home. She'd hold up a slender feather, brown on top but bright yellow underneath. "Yellow shafted flicker," she'd announce. "See, that's why it's called that. The shafts of its feathers are yellow. Pretty, eh?" I was presented with abandoned nests, wounded birds, salamanders. I'd make her take them outside, but she'd sneak them back in. Or she'd build shelters to house them outside. She would bug me and bug me to come out and look at something; it was always easier to relent. Once a luna moth sunning at the edge of Grace's garden. Such a colour of green I'd never seen before. The green of Eden, I imagined.

She told me about watching a turtle excavate a hole with its back feet and deposit into it eighteen eggs the size and shape of ping-pong balls, then cover it up and drag itself back into the pond. She marked the spot and returned every day for weeks, hoping to see the newly hatched young emerge.

Once she brought a crinkly bit of light-coloured paper home, asked me to guess what it was. "Look at the shape. See how it's kind of a tube?"

Still no idea.

"A snake's skin—the skin it shed when it moulted."

She read the look on my face. "When they grow, they have to shed their old skin, otherwise they can't grow. Interesting, eh?" She fingered the frail paper in her hand. "I wonder how it starts. I guess the new skin must form underneath, so the old skin dries out. Imagine what that feels like, to have a second layer of skin form underneath your outer skin—must feel weird, eh? Like wearing two pairs of leather gloves. I bet it feels tight, till the new skin dries out enough to come off. Imagine crawling right out of your skin! Or having a zipper— zIIIIP!—open up the skin on your belly, peel it off your arms and legs, and step out wearing..." Her clumsy pirouette. "A brand new skin!"

Another time she came home with an empty wasp nest, the grey paper torn to reveal the many tiny cells inside. Hexagons, she told me. All of those cells were identically sized hexagons. Otherwise it would never form a perfect round globe. "And d'you know how they make paper?" she asked me. "The wasps chew up wood fibre and spit it out; then they somehow make those tiny walls with it. I can't figure out how they get the spit-up to make the walls." She placed the torn nest in my palm. It was light as air, perfect hexagons built from wasp spit. I tried to picture the insects manipulating the regurgitated pulp, building each wall of the many cells, each one the same length, adding one hexagon onto another.

"What are the cells for?"

"It's where the eggs go. The queen lays one egg in each cell, and then the workers look after the larvae after they're born."

"The larvae?"

"That's the first stage. Before it becomes a wasp, it's like a little worm. The workers feed it, and it grows and pupates, like caterpillars do, and when it's ready, ta-da! It comes out of the pupa as an adult wasp. That's called metamorphosis, when it starts out as one thing and then changes into something else."

When Grace announced that summer that she was going to make paper, I didn't protest, especially since she clarified that she wouldn't be using her own saliva to do it. But she couldn't make paper as fine as the wasps did. She tried building an oversized wasp nest, managed seven cells before giving up. She wouldn't throw it away, though; she coated it with shellac and fastened it to the trunk of the maple tree in the front yard.

One day she took me down to the river to watch a dragonfly emerge from its larva. I had no idea that this large-headed insect with the long gossamer wings began its existence as a small, ugly thing that lived in the water. Grace found one that had crawled out of the river and was resting on the sand. The nymph, she called it—an unlikely name given its appearance: about an inch long, stubby, looking as if it was made of armour, something hammered into shape on an anvil. But it was soft. As we watched, something very bizarre started to happen. The skin on the nymph's back, which was drying out, began to tear ever so slightly. Something was moving around in there, pushing through the skin. Just behind the nymph's head, another head was emerging, with two huge eyes.

It was almost terrible to watch—the terrible wonder of it, this creature emerging from within the skin of another, within the being of another. What kind of thing could harbour this inside it? And at what point did it stop being a nymph and begin to be something else?

The dragonfly's emergence was slow and halting, as if it was struggling against exhaustion, or maybe it was cramped and stiff—understandably, since the adult was almost three times as long as the nymph it was stuffed inside. Eventually we could see its legs fumbling through the ripped skin as the dragonfly crept out of the nymph and perched on its back. It took another long while for its long, slender tail to untuck itself and for its wings to come unstuck from its body. "It has to sit here till its wings dry out," Grace explained, "before it's ready to fly. I wonder how that nymph knew it was time to come out of the water. Did it have any idea what was going to happen to it? What a shock, to have your body taken over like that, like an alien invasion or something!"

Her face, when she talked like that. Her round, shining face, eyes blue like mine.

But so unlike mine.

Water in my cup. I drank tentatively, guardedly. Not wanting to deplete it, not sure if more would flow into it.

Maggie

"SPOKEN WORD?" MAGGIE CHUCKLES. "As opposed to unspoken word, a word that's just thought but not stated?"

"Oh stop, you know about this, don't you? It's kind of a cross be-tween a poetry reading and drama—a poetry performance." Leyla reads the expression on Maggie's face. "It'll be interesting! It's part of this festival, stuff going on all over the place." She laughs. "Come on, be brave—broaden your horizons a bit."

It's a small venue, a café with a low platform across one end of the room. A woman stands alone on the stage, which is dark but for a single light shining down on her from above. Her head is lowered, and her hands are at her sides. Slowly she raises one arm, seems to be unfurling it. The other arm does the same; then both hands are reaching all around her, groping about in the air as if she's searching for something. Her head gradually lifts, too, as she says,

No one here.

One hand, in its circling search, accidentally bumps against her chest. She flinches in surprise, then begins patting her torso all over as if to verify its existence.

Oh. Heh heh.

I am.

(I think.)

She drops her hands to her sides.

Of course.

Begins striding around the stage.

> *It's me. Fully present!*

Stands at attention, saluting.

> *Here, sir! Yes, sir! Present, sir!*

Her eyes move about wildly as the rest of her is at attention, still saluting, but gradually the salute sags into a hand shading her eyes, and she's squinting, searching.

> *Sir?*

She takes a deep breath; her face shows hopelessness. She sighs. In a self-conscious way, she starts humming, scratching her elbow and her knee. Then she straightens up, looks around vaguely.

> *I'm here.*

Peers into the darkness again, hand shading her eyes.

> *Me and my voice.*
>
> *Hello!*
>
> *Heh heh.*
>
> *It is mine, isn't it?*
>
> *Hello!*
>
> *Heh heh. Yup, it's mine.*

She stands still a moment, silenced by something that has just occurred to her.

> *But what should I*
> *say?*

Looks skyward, then around, waiting for an answer. Sighs.

> *Not getting much help here.*

Silly laughter. Flippantly, says

> *Whatever comes into my head, then!*

She stops, feels her head, her throat. Opens and closes her mouth. Then, in a loud, drawn out whisper:

> *Wwwoooorrrrddddsss*

Repeats, a bit louder, slowly drawing out each letter. Then:

> *I can talk about wwoorrddss.*

Stops and thinks.

    Surely not
    just
    words
    but something else too

Inhales, and on slow exhale says

    the breath
    that cradles them

Faces the audience square-on, and enunciates sharply:

    or expells them—
    projectiles fired across any distance
    even celestial:

Stands feet splayed, arms straight at sides, hands in fists, head tilted back, shouts

    insults hurled at God!

Listens for a response, then gradually releases herself from that stance.

    Hmph.

    We think words originate
    here [places a finger against her temple]

    We picture
    neat, ordered packages

    Or starched soldiers
    marching into the world
    in long lines broken only by
    appropriate punctuation

Draws exaggerated punctuation marks in the air with index finger.

    But it's not so neat and tidy, no—
    words travel with
    blood

Finding Grace

though sometimes they bypass
the heart
Hand makes wide circles around the heart
and travel through
fists instead
Both hands make sudden fists; she holds that pose a moment, then
gradually loosens, shakes it off.
Sometimes too, words become...
amorphous [mimes wilting]

as imprecise as Dali timepieces
wilting in imponderable landscapes

Sometimes words swim [continues miming as she speaks]
sometimes they flow like a river
then go
plunging
over a precipice

We want words to carry us safely across
all those gorges
a solid bridge, not a ropy affair
swinging wildly beneath our weight.

We want something
engineered
with sturdy mathematical equations behind it
Begins pacing, fingers on chin, mulling over a problem
But more than that too—not just
numbers
but a calculus of the heart.

How else will it span the chasm?
But how to construct
that bridge?
What words can be ratcheted together
to span the distance between oneself and another...
between you
and me?

Points alternately to audience and self, as she repeats slowly:

Between you
and me?
Between you
and me?

Uses facial expression and mime throughout the following:

The dropped words cause the most trouble
all those missing words
the awkward ones, the hardest to vocalize.
If we were to string all those fallen words
together in a sentence or a book
what a weighty tome we'd have.

But listen to me—all these words! [Laughs]
Too many! [Laughs]
That's the other end of the spectrum:
all the extra words—
the unnecessary ones
or those meant to muddy the waters,
distract us.
Compliments and lies and
threats of damnation.

Finding Grace

No wonder we have such trouble finding our way.
The words we need most are not just words, but
sustenance: bread and water.
Or bread and wine, something consecrated:
a prayer, a benediction.

Or parachutes: [hand mimes drifting parachute]
Something to ease us down lightly into the darkness
and wings [hand mimes wings lifting]
to carry us out again.

Mimes parachute and wings again, saying

down into darkness

and out again…

She looks up, skyward or heavenward, hands shade eyes as she searches. Then she sighs. Repeats motion of hand as parachute and then as wings, as the light fades.

When the lights come up after the performance, Maggie stares wide-eyed at Leyla, who says, "I know—you're speechless, right?" They both laugh.

"I am," says Maggie. "It seems silly to try to say anything about it. Just: wow. It was kind of goofy at times, and yet so…true."

Leyla nods.

"Amazing how she could say so much, so clearly. She nailed it way better than a psych text," chuckles Maggie.

"Poetry usually does."

"You know, I was drawn to psychology because I thought it might explain a few things—why people behave the way they do. Why I am the way I am. So in Intro Psych, we covered 'the communication process.' They have all these models and diagrams. The sender, the receiver, the message, the noise, the feedback loop—all these things in neat boxes. I find myself resisting those types of models, all the boxes with lines and arrows linking one to another. It's messier than that. It *is* more like what this woman just did. I'd like to see a psychologist put what she did into boxes!"

"But are you enjoying the psych program? Is it a good fit for you?"

"Overall, yes. And it's better somehow going to school full time—easier to get into it than when I was taking one course at a time." Maggie rolls her eyes. "Even though I still feel like a grandmother, in class with all those twenty-year-olds."

Leyla grins. "Mid-thirties isn't quite grandmother age—although I'm sure those twenty-year-olds think you're ancient."

"And some days I feel it. I'll be glad to finish up in another year and a half."

"Then what?"

"I'm not sure. What does anybody do with a psych degree?"

"Graduate work."

"Oh God."

"Focus your research on the communication process. Become a doctor of psychology and fix the broken models."

"Ha ha."

Leyla wags a finger at her. "Don't just close the door on possibilities."

Grace

"WHAT DID MY FATHER LOOK LIKE?"

Iris was at the sink, washing dishes. Her hands paused, then resumed.

Grace, nineteen years old, was drying a metal bowl. "Do you have any pictures of him?"

"I don't think so."

"What did he look like? Do I take after him?"

Iris studied her daughter, the round face and fair hair, the sturdy body, her wide hands, short fingers cradling the bowl as she peered at the side of it, moving it toward her face and then away. "No. You look more like me."

Grace brought the side of the bowl up close to her face again. "Was his nose as big as mine looks in this bowl?"

Grace often caught Iris like this; a chuckle she didn't know was there escaped, leaving an open door behind it. "He had dark hair and brown eyes."

"Tall, dark and handsome?"

"Short. But handsome."

"I wish there was a picture." She put the bowl down, picked up a metal pot, too scratched to be a mirror. "What about Margaret?"

A kick in the stomach. Iris stopped breathing. The letter *M* stalled on her lips.

"Maggie. The Humphries told me about her."

Iris ran the tap, thoroughly rinsed the frying pan.

"What did they say?"

"Mr. Humphries taught her one semester. That's when she started calling herself Maggie instead of Margaret. He said she didn't like math."

Did I know she didn't like math? What did I know of her?

"They said she moved away before finishing high school. Where did she go?"

"I don't know."

"She never came back, she never visited?"

"No."

"Why?"

"I don't know."

"She never said where she was going?"

"She said she didn't know."

"How can you go somewhere if you don't know where it is?"

No reply.

"So she doesn't know about me?"

"No."

"Do I look like her?"

Iris turned toward Grace, studied her face again. "No. She looked like your father."

"Maybe we could find her. Maybe she'd like to know she has a sister."

Iris drained the water from the sink, squeezed out the dishrag. "There's a lot of Whites in the phone books."

Maggie leaving, not knowing where she was going. Going anywhere, going nowhere.

An old door leaned against the stone wall of the basement. A perfect round hole in it where the doorknob was. Blue paint on it peeling and worn. Grace didn't repaint it. She built a frame to house the door, then got Kaia and Eric to help her dig posts into the ground in the side yard. They nailed the frame to the posts, and then hung the door in the frame, using hinges that let it swing both ways in the wind.

It opened, closed, opened, admitting nothing but the wind, dead leaves, seeds on the wing.

It opened but there was nobody there. And it closed again.

It was an old broken door that wouldn't latch. But that was why it was always opening.

Kaia admired the new installation. "What does your mother think about it?"

"She thinks I'm messing up the yard with old junk. But I haven't told her the name of it yet."

Maggie

JAMILA FINDS OUT FROM MAGGIE THE DATE of her graduation. "I am putting it on the calendar. We are going to have a big party!" She frowns. "But the end of May is one month away. Aren't you finishing exams, everything, now?"

"Yes, thank God. I'll be done next Thursday."

"Okay! We must also have a celebration sooner—a small, relaxing one. A weekend—our friend has a cottage he wants us to use. This is the perfect time, just after you finish all your hard work. Do you want to?"

It's just Jamila and Maggie who go to the lake three hours north of Toronto for the weekend. Leyla is attending a conference, Amal is busy with the kids, and Fareed doesn't know what he would do there. "Sitting beside a lake all the day? You two go, enjoy yourselves. It will be good for Jamila—you need a rest, so tired lately."

Maggie has noticed it, too: Jamila's unusual pallor and fatigue. She convinces her to take a holiday even from cooking on the weekend, so they bring packaged food from the grocery store—frozen pizza, canned soup, bottled sauce for pasta. They laugh as Jamila bemoans this decision; not only does the food taste terrible, but it gives her heartburn. "You are a bad influence, Maggie, thinking to bring this ... this food that is not food!"

They're sitting on a bare rock that slopes down to the lake. The landscape is startlingly familiar to Maggie. Startling because she didn't think any of it had made an impression on her when she lived in Barret River. The reddish-brown rock cuts along the highway as they drove up here, and the sculpted pines. The sound of the wind through those pines—she listens to it now, a mournful, faraway sound.

She comments to Jamila that the place reminds her of where she grew up.

"Tell me about that place." Jamila's large brown eyes.

"Big trees like these—not everywhere, but around. Especially down at the lake. Lake Superior—it's more like an ocean, really. Rocky shore like here."

"You grew up in a place as beautiful as this?"

"Well, the town wasn't so beautiful. But the river was nice; it ran through the town and then through the mill area—and after that it wasn't so nice any more."

"The mill where your father worked?"

Maggie leans back, hands resting on the warm rock, and stretches her legs out in front of her. "Yeah."

Jamila has tried in the past to learn about Maggie's parents, but could never get her to talk much about them. "What was he like?"

Maggie looks at Jamila, sighs. "I didn't see him much. He drank a lot."

Jamila nods. "And your mother?"

"My mother was very religious—Pentecostal, strict. My father never behaved the way she wanted him to. They fought a lot."

"How old were you when your mother died?"

Maggie turns her head toward the water, flames dancing on its surface from the sun. She pulls her knees up to her chest, wraps her arms around them. "My mother never had a heart attack, Jamila. And my father didn't die of an aneurism. I made that up."

Jamila's eyes widen. "They are still living?"

"I don't know, probably."

"You don't know?" She looks down, then back at Maggie. "You don't know?"

Maggie takes a deep breath and exhales slowly. "You wouldn't understand, Jamila. It wasn't a family like your family. My parents were…they were both screwed up. I had to get out of that house, and I did. If I'd stayed, it would have been like being buried. And since I left, they have both been dead to me."

"You left… You never phoned your mother, or wrote to her… They don't know where you are?"

Maggie says nothing.

"She is your mother. He is your father. You are their daughter."

"She was a religious fanatic, not a mother."

"But still—"

"Jamila, you have been far more of a mother to me than she was. She didn't know how to be a mother."

"Maybe that was not her fault, maybe she was trying."

Maggie shifts her legs, crosses her arms. "It doesn't matter. I've got along fine, which is more than I likely would have done had I stayed."

"How many years since you left?"

"Almost twenty-two years."

Jamila is quiet for a few minutes. "I think about one of my daughters disappearing, for over twenty years… I can not imagine."

"That's because you *are* a mother, Jamila. You know how to love like a mother. That was not my mother."

They are both silent for a while.

"All my mother cared about was religion, what the preacher said, how we were supposed to think and act. She didn't love me, or my father, for whatever reason. She didn't need me; she had her church. My father was a good-for-nothing drunk. And for me, being there was like being strangled. So why would I stick around?" Maggie tries to chuckle. "My mother was a bit psycho, actually."

After a minute, Jamila asserts, "A mother is a mother. If you have children some day, you will know."

Maggie laughs. "I'm not about to start having children now, Jamila, at age thirty-eight."

But Jamila is not in a mood for laughter.

Iris

THE YARD WAS GETTING TO BE A CRAZY MESS. Grace glided around my complaints and just kept adding things. I got used to the painted shoes lining the walk, the hands and ears made out of plaster showing up here and there as if the yard was a garbage dump for severed body parts. The ear is almost like a shell, she said; maybe that's why it hears the sea when you hold a shell up to it. Where she got these crazy ideas I never knew, but she was always delighting herself with them.

And me.

But one day it wasn't exactly delight, it was something else she stirred in me—the day she hung a door in the frame she'd made. Out there on the lawn, a door standing in the middle of nowhere. The effort she'd gone to, digging posts into the ground to hold the frame in place. Kaia and Eric helped, but still. All that just to put an old wrecked door out there, a door going nowhere. After they were done, I went out to have a look. Grace was standing in front of it, admiring it. She caught my eye, then pushed the door. It swung open one way and then the other. It wouldn't even stay closed; there was no knob or latch. Just a door, swinging in the air, lonely looking.

Maggie

FAREED AND MAGGIE ARE BOTH IN THE OFFICE when the phone call comes. Then they're dashing out the door, flying for the car. Fareed is mumbling as he drives, but Maggie can't hear what he's saying, her ears are jammed, her head filled with a loud drone. Fingers gripping the door handle, right foot ramming the floorboards as she tries to brake each time they nearly collide with another vehicle. It takes hours, weeks, months to reach the hospital. At the emergency department they're led to a small room with a curtain across the door. Leyla's on this side of the gurney, Amal is on the other. Maggie hangs back as Fareed rushes to the bedside. He cups Jamila's face in his palms, strokes her forehead, smooths back her hair, all the while his deep voice climbing high and then breaking; waves and waves of words cresting and breaking over Jamila's still body. Leyla has her arm around her father's back, and when he rests his head on Jamila's chest, Amal and Leyla both lean in, embracing their parents and each other. Maggie stands two steps away, her eyes unable to stray from a shadow, a hint of flesh where the sheet covering Jamila has almost fallen away from her foot. The electric jabbering in Maggie's head increases, buzzing down her spine, into her gut, dismembering her arms and legs. Eventually Leyla turns to her, extends an arm to bring her into the circle. Jamila's face. Her mouth sagging open, the dark cave of it. The shape of yearning: a mouth that's asking for more, and more, and more.

Finding Grace

Maggie has never been to a funeral home before, or any kind of funeral service. She looks at the figure lying in the casket, hands clasped across the abdomen. The short fingers with their familiar, small nails are wrong somehow. Maggie wants to lift the fingertips to her nose, sniff for a hint of garlic to see if it's really Jamila. Her cheeks, her whole face heavily powdered—Jamila never wore makeup. The colour is wrong, the powder too pale. Or unable to cover up what's beneath it: alabaster, cold stone. Maggie starts to panic. What did they do with her blood, her warm flesh? What did they do with Jamila? The laughter that was her eyes, the love that was her arms. Even the yearning that was her mouth at the end—how did they make it close, seal off the *more* it was asking for? Maggie's jaw is clenched and her lungs too; she can't breathe. Then she's gasping for air and reaching, prodding the figure in the casket that once was Jamila but is no longer.

Jamila is gone.

Maggie falls into the well of her absence.

Grace

HER MOTHER HAD BEEN FEELING SICK FOR SOME TIME before the lump appeared. On the day Iris learned that she didn't have much time left, Grace came home from work and found Mrs. Baxter at the house.

"Gracey, honey, your mother is going soon, to be with the Lord. He's calling her to come home." Mrs. Baxter always talked like that, like any minute the Lord would walk in the door or call on the phone.

In the bedroom, Iris was lying on top of the blankets, staring at the ceiling. She turned her head to face her daughter.

"Did Mrs. Baxter tell you?"

"Yes. She told me. She said the Lord is calling you."

Blue eyes on the ceiling again.

"What does it sound like?"

"Sound like?" she frowned.

"When he calls. What do you hear?"

Iris sighed, looked out the window as October leaves sailed past. "Your sister…"

Grace waited. She didn't want to say anything that might jam up the words.

"Don't sell the house. In case she comes back."

Sunlight outside the windows was sieved through an invisible filter, making the air in the hospital grey. The grey crept beneath everyone's skin and into their eyes. Even healthy people looked grey. The IV machine emitted thin beeps at regular intervals, softer than the loud

190

beep blaring down the hall, calling a nurse to someone's bedside. Constant hallway noise of wheels rolling on concrete: carts, trolleys, stretchers. Bustling nurses' shoes, shuffling patient slippers. And everywhere a vague odour of bodily fluids and decay lurking beneath a broader chemical smell.

The elderly woman in the next bed was hard of hearing. Her son yelled into her ear. HOW ARE YOU FEELING TODAY, MAMA? DID THEY BRING YOU LUNCH? A sparrow's voice answered. WHAT'S THAT? YELLOW WHAT? Another peep. OH, JELLO—YOU HAD JELLO?

Grace sat on the blue vinyl chair beside her mother's bed, watched yellow-orange fluid drip into the bag hanging from the lower bed rail. She wondered what the death would look like. Whether her mother would slide into stillness or grope for oxygen, whether she was even at that moment willing her heart to keep pushing the blood. What would make it stop? The nurse had said her organs would gradually shut down, the heart being the last to go. She pictured the heart in there, a fist opening and closing, never pausing until one day it had had enough.

Enough, or not enough? Had her mother had enough?

Iris's forehead creased. Her fingers fluttered, her breathing's rhythm became interrupted. She jerked her head from side to side, called out one word: Eleanor. Then she was jabbering, the sentences slurred, incomprehensible. After a few minutes, she settled into sleep again. Grace studied her mother's face. The mouth sagging open a bit, the flesh along her jaw drooping into jowls. The downy blonde hair that softened the side of her cheek just in front of the ear, and the longer hairs curling from her chin. She thought about making a mask of her mother's face, wondered how she could do it. Plaster of Paris, lots of vaseline on her skin first?

No point in asking her.

Besides, a mask couldn't capture those baby-silk hairs on her cheeks, or the coarser ones on her chin—the things that made her mother look vulnerable, young and old at the same time. So what would have been the point? It would have just been a mask of a face.

Kaia went to the hospital with Grace the day the nurse phoned to say it was time. They sat alongside Iris's bed, watched her chest rise and fall, each breath a gasp in through the open mouth and a loud sigh out. Occasional pauses occurred in her breathing; with each pause, Grace and Kaia leaned forward in their chairs, their own breathing stalled, until the dying woman's chest rose again with another intake of air. The pauses became more frequent and the spaces between each breath longer, until all that was left was the pause itself, and time going on and on.

The depth of that pause, that held-breath ending. Like an ocean swell suspended, the volume of the entire ocean pushing up against it. Grace could feel the pressure of it, that density, pushing against her own lungs, and thought she might stop breathing herself. But after a few days, the suspended wave let go and the pressure in her chest subsided, though it was replaced with a kind of hollow: more space there than she was used to.

Emptiness in other ways, too. Like ghost pain in an amputated limb: the physical pain that's felt in the very limb that's gone, felt right in the place it used to be. It throbs so much you want to massage it, but all that's there is air. There was an ache like that in the house, and everything at home sounded different, too. So odd—how a house can sound different when someone who is usually there isn't there any more. Even someone as quiet as her mother. And how the sound changed now that her mother was gone for good, compared to when she'd just gone off to work for the day, or out for groceries. Now, when Grace walked in and closed the door behind her, the sound of the door clicking shut was amplified somehow, as if something was an-nouncing: This Is The Sound Of A Door Closing. And the thump of Grace's sock feet on the bare floor. Each footfall an echo. Even voices on the radio seemed wayward, directionless, as if they were flailing about in an empty room, searching for a certain set of eardrums. And there was something behind all those other sounds: something that went on and on, that magnified all the others. It was sort of a sound itself, but not exactly. It was both a presence and an absence at the same time. An aural shadow.

So she'd play the Audubon Society CD she had for identifying bird songs and calls. The house would fill with the nasal beeps of nighthawks and woodcocks, the gravelly croak of a sandhill crane, the swamp-pump gulping of an American bittern, and the ululations of the boreal owl.

"What about what your mother wanted—did she ever say?" Kaia asked as they headed to their appointment at the funeral home. "Did she want a regular funeral, at the church?"

"I don't know. We never talked about it."

"So if she didn't tell you anything, if she hasn't written it down anywhere—it's up to you to decide."

"Yeah." But Grace was distracted by the idea of embalming. She was picturing lab specimens from her high school biology class, frogs and worms pickled in formaldehyde. The idea of doing that to people seemed odd. And once the embalmed body went into the ground, how long was it preserved there? All the worms, bacteria and fungi responsible for breaking down organic matter—would they avoid a formaldehyde-laced corpse like they would a toxic waste dump? She pictured them nibbling on a finger or a toe until they realized what was inside. Whoa! Let's get out of here, they'd say as they wriggled away.

Cruel rejection, when a worm didn't want anything to do with you! But it wouldn't matter what a person was like when alive—no matter how friendly or smart or fashionable. Once they were down there smelling of mothballs, they'd all be the same: repulsive to the soil organisms that would otherwise be drawn to them.

"What about you," Kaia was saying, "would you like your mother to have a church funeral?"

There'd be music, and the pastor would be all happy about Iris going home to Jesus, talking about how they would see her again in heaven. But that image of her in the hospital bed—the hollows beneath her cheekbones, how large her teeth looked in a face that had been wasting away. Heaven would be a pretty gruesome place if we all looked like we did at the moment of our death. But with all the magic involved in the idea of heaven, God would have figured out how to make us more presentable. And anyway, by the sounds of it, everyone would be so happy and relieved to be there that they wouldn't give a hoot how anybody looked.

"She'll want to go to heaven."

After a moment, Kaia said, "Yes. She will."

"If I don't have a church funeral, will she get there?"

"I don't know." Then, "Maybe at this point it's what you would like. Whatever makes you feel better."

"The singing is nice."

The church women brought egg salad sandwiches and squares, poured coffee in the downstairs lounge. The person in the casket was a stranger; her mother was already long gone. The songs were as boisterous as usual, everyone had similar words to say about heaven and Jesus, the pastor and Grace tossed clots of dirt down onto the casket in the ground. How long before that shiny, lacquered wood rots? How long before she really returns to dust?

Funny how that thought was the most wondrous one, her mother's body eventually disintegrating, the molecular compounds that made up flesh and bone coming apart so that all that was left were her constituent elements: carbon, calcium, oxygen, and so on.

In the days following the funeral, she kept thinking about this. About how the human body was made of millions of atoms and molecules arranged in such a way that they formed skin, cartilage, skull, pancreas. And all of it started with a defined number of elements, the ones listed in the Periodic Table of Elements she'd learned about in chemistry. The chart in her dictionary listed 103 elements, a finite storehouse of building blocks. Like the pieces in a Lego set: there were only so many types, but you could arrange them in an almost infinite number of ways. And just as variety in Lego pieces increased over the years, scientists had been discovering more elements. You could see they'd been having fun naming some of the newer ones, like Californium and Berkelium. There was even one called Einsteinium, and its atomic number was 99. The Gretzky of elements!

It was amusing to think of everyone being constructed of something that sounded as mundane as carbon, magnesium, potassium and selenium. As if we were all just big, animate multivitamins. Imagine using x-ray vision, seeing through people's skin to a schema representing the molecular compounds that we're composed of. What would the schema for the heart be? Or the brain? She chuckled. For some people, it might just be *He* plain and simple: helium for brains. At least they'd be stable, since helium was one of the few elements that didn't have electrons trying to fly off and mate with some other element. Come to think of it, it made perfect sense that we were mostly made of unstable elements, with atoms scurrying around trying to ally themselves with others; elements that weren't happy just being what they were, that were always trying to become something else. It explained a lot about human behaviour. Who needed psychology? Maybe all we needed were analytic chemists to put people in touch with their inner selves. Their very deep inner selves.

But the Periodic Table couldn't explain everything. There was something else we were made of that wasn't explained by chemistry. What about emotion? Maybe it was just chemistry and physics, too. Like water coming to a boil—when it was heated, the molecules sped up and ran around in more and more of a frenzy. Maybe emotion was just a version of that. People talked about their blood boiling, about someone blowing up in anger. He really blew a gasket. She was just blowing off steam. Or someone cried hysterically, had a paroxysm of tears.

And what about when people at church got so filled up with the Holy Spirit they spoke in tongues? Was that chemistry too? The Spirit causing a chemical reaction, like sunlight does in plants. Which of the elements that might be in a person was the one that responded to the spirit's light? Lead?

Did it turn the lead to gold?

Iris

THAT LONELY-LOOKING DOOR IN THE MIDDLE of the lawn. Grace
caught my eye and pushed it open. After it swung one way, the wind
caught it and pushed it back in the other direction. It stayed like that,
wide open, as if it was waiting for someone to step through.

I was starting to turn back to the house when she told me what
she called it.

Maggie

YOU CAME FROM A PLACE AS BEAUTIFUL AS THIS? She can hear Jamila's voice as she drives past long sand beaches bordered by rocky headlands jutting into the blue, and then inland through forest, where small ponds mirror green trees. The wide lake eventually reappears through the trees or from atop the steep hills the highway has to climb on its way to Thunder Bay. She's not going that far, though.

Before she reaches the Barret River turnoff, she pulls into a roadside picnic area next to a small river that spills over rocky shelves and then meanders into a wide, still pool. All along the edge of the water is bald rock, scoured by the force that the river gathers during spring runoff. Polished whales lounging on the river's edge. Maggie sits on the rock, watching the water go on its way, clear and detached. Not wistful. It swirls unconcerned around and through obstructions in its path, drowned trees whose upended roots snag dead leaves and twigs but not the river itself. She runs her hands over the smooth granite and wonders how something unconscious of where and how it flows can have this effect, wear the rough edges down to a satin finish. The landscape shapes the river, it's true, but the river also alters the land it passes through. And it does so almost imperceptibly, bit by bit, through time. Just by being itself.

The road in from the highway is shorter than she remembers; it takes about half an hour to reach the town. She crosses the railroad and passes the sprawling paper mill. Upstream from the mill, the main street parallels the river. When she left, the downtown covered a narrow grid of five or six blocks along Water Street. It doesn't seem to have grown any, but it looks better overall. The sidewalks seem wider, and trees have been planted along the main street. Colourful murals cover the outer walls of several buildings, and many of the storefronts are brightly painted: deep mauve, fuchsia, sky blue. There's even an outdoor patio along the side of what used to be the Peacock Garden restaurant, which has a new name, something Mediterranean sounding. She catches a glimpse of an outdoor equipment or outfitter's shop in the next block, but the car on her tail makes her speed up. She doesn't know what to do first: pull over and explore the downtown on foot, or drive on to her old neighbourhood at the edge of town. She's not sure whether she's ready for that yet, but decides not to procrastinate.

She turns onto her old street, drives slowly past the house. Notices the strange lawn ornaments, is that what they are? Decides to park further down the street and wander back.

Lining the walkway to the front door are sneakers painted violet, scarlet, lime green, sun yellow. A doorframe and door stand in the middle of the lawn, connected to nothing, the door swinging vaguely in the breeze. Large stones painted with faces lie about in the grass. Copper pipes and wires have been twisted into the shape of a tree; from the curling branches hang various items: a braid of hair, a ruined sock, a large-baubled costume-bead necklace, a raven feather. A dead tree has been planted upside down, its roots forming a stunted canopy.

Maggie pauses on the sidewalk as she's taking all this in. What weirdos live here now, she wonders. When did my parents leave, or are they both dead? The front door opens and a young woman emerges, wearing an orange and green striped shirt, orange pants and orange sneakers. The woman descends the front steps, and when she sees Maggie standing on the road, she barks out a hello.

Maggie, awkward now, says hello, starts to move away but hesitates. "I used to live here so I just came by to have a look."

The woman stares at her. "In this house? Did you live in this house, or do you mean the neighbourhood?" She begins down the walkway toward Maggie.

"In this house. I lived in your house."

Something in Grace's stomach jumps, like a fish breaking the surface of the river. She stops, peers at the ground and then at the visitor. "When did you live here?"

"I left a long time ago—over twenty years. When did you move in?"

Grace pauses, squinting up at the sky. Then she looks directly at Maggie and says, "I've always lived here."

Maggie is startled by this. The woman appears to be in her twenties.

"Well here," says the young woman, motioning toward the yard with a wave of her arm. "Do you want to look around? You can look around if you want. I don't mind. Lots of people are curious about all my stuff here, especially people from away, they like to come and have a look."

"Um, okay, if you don't mind. It's kind of interesting." She takes a few steps along the walkway, gazing down at the brightly painted sneakers lining it. "Did you do all this?"

"Yeah," the woman laughs, a nervous trill. "That's what everyone asks, I don't know why. I don't know who else they think does it."

"Does everybody also ask *why* you do it? I mean, why painted running shoes along the front walk?"

"Some ask, but most look like they want to ask but they don't." She chuckles. "Maybe they don't want to hear the answer, maybe they're afraid of what I might say."

"Well I'm intrigued enough to ask. Whatever possessed you to do all this?"

"I don't know. It's just something I do."

"Not a very scary answer."

"Maybe that's why people don't ask," she grins. "Maybe they know the answer would be a let-down."

Maggie spies the last of this season's irises, fading in a small garden beneath the front window. "Did you plant those?"

"Yup."

Maggie's thinking how ironic that is as they wander over to have a closer look. Then she notices that the edge of the flower bed is covered with eyeballs—small round stones painted to resemble eyeballs, each one with an iris and pupil surrounded by lightly veined white. On some of them, eyelids and lashes have also been painted; others are simply naked eyeballs. Maggie's breath catches in her throat at first, and she gapes at the woman. Then from deep in her belly a slow laugh rumbles out. She inhales and sighs, looks back at the bed of eyeballs, smiling and shaking her head. If only her mother could see what this woman has done right here in the front yard. She would think an exorcism was required.

"Not many people laugh when they see this," says the woman.

"It's wonderful. So eerie." They smile at one another.

Something hanging in a nearby tree catches Maggie's eye, and she moves toward it: a ghost-like form suspended from a branch. It's a translucent sculpture made of fibreglass cloth and clear resin. A ragged, life-sized human figure—or partial figure: no legs; just head, arms, and torso, though not even those parts are complete. A wide gap flays the right side, a long jagged tear from the right shoulder down and across the belly. The arms stretch out to the sides but are also incomplete; shoulders and biceps are clearly formed, but the rest of the arms dissolve. The head is thrown back. Neck, chin, cheekbones, nose and forehead are intact; the rest of the head appears to have disintegrated. But the thrust-back head, the outstretched arms and arched torso are what give this form life. Especially the chin and neck, the bulge of the larynx and on either side of it the slight depression framed by ridges of muscle. The clavicle at the base of the neck, with its ridges and hollows. This is where the detail is clearest, most complete: the contours of the jaw, the chin thrust up and forward, the vulnerable, exposed neck.

Is it ecstasy or anguish, Maggie isn't sure; it's so luminous and yet so torn. Leaf shadows dance all through it as it sways lightly in the breeze. It's who or what we are at our core: fragile yet resilient, temporal yet immortal bits of light.

She finds herself crying, holding a hand up to her mouth, glancing at the woman, embarrassed but unable to stop. "I'm sorry," she whispers.

"It's okay."

"It's just… it reminds me of somebody. Hard to explain."

"I know. My friend Kaia made this. I told her I was thinking about making a plaster mask of my mother's face when she was dying, but figured it wouldn't work, wouldn't do what I wanted it to. Kaia's been making these sculptures and asked if I wanted to hang one out here. It's way better than a plaster mask would have been."

"So this makes you think of your mother?"

"Yeah. And everybody, sort of."

Maggie wipes her eyes, looks at the woman and then at the figure again. "Yes. All of us." And after a moment: "Tell me again how long you've lived here?"

Maggie's Door

THEN SHE TOLD ME WHAT SHE CALLED IT, the door that admitted nothing and everything.

Where does your breath go in moments like that, as if a hand reached into your chest and squeezed your lungs tight. When you breathe again it's like the first breath you ever took, having just emerged from your mother's womb. Or the first breath of wind after the earth was made, testing the limits of the sky.

About the Author

Mary-Lynn Murphy lives north of Sault Ste. Marie, Ontario, in the community of Goulais River. Her poetry has appeared in several Canadian literary magazines. *Finding Grace* is her first novel.